THE DOG IN THE FREEZER

three novellas by

· H A R R Y M A Z E R ·

ALADDIN PAPERBACKS

For my sister-in-law, Linda Fox, who still kisses dogs. She inspires me with her explosive laugh, her enthusiasm, and her love of all animals.

* * *

First Aladdin Paperbacks edition September 1998

Copyright © 1997 by Harry Mazer. "Giles' Song" by Gina Mazer; copyright © 1997 by Gina Mazer. Used by permission of the author.

Aladdin Paperbacks
An imprint of Simon & Schuster Children's Publishing Division
1230 Avenue of the Americas
New York, NY 10020

Designed by Heather Wood
The text for this book was set in Bembo.
Printed and bound in the United States of America
10 9 8 7 6 5 4 3 2 1

The Library of Congress has cataloged the hardcover edition as follows:
Mazer, Harry.
The dog in the freezer : three novellas / by Harry Mazer
p.   cm.
Summary: Each of these three novellas looks at the relationship between
a boy and a dog in a very different and unusual way.
ISBN 0-689-80753-8 (hc.)
[1. Dogs—Fiction.] I. Title.
PZ7.M47397Di   1997   [Fic]—dc21
96-44833
CIP   AC
ISBN 0-689-80754-6 (pbk.)

CONTENTS

THE DOG IN THE FREEZER

three novellas

MY LIFE AS A BOY

1 ◎ **It happened to me.** To me and Gregory. You can believe it or not, but this is a true story. I was in a dog run in an SPCA facility when I first saw him. I had found myself a little shade and was watching the Sunday afternoon gawkers, parents and their kids lined up oohing and aahing over the cute little pups. Nobody was interested in a mature dog. I didn't expect to find a new family too soon.

My old family had gone overseas and left me here, because there was no place for me in their plans. I don't think this is the time to go into the whole story of my life, because it's Gregory I want to tell you about, but I've seen a thing or two, and I've had some bad experiences.

What does a dog want? Being a dog I've thought about it a lot. A dog wants to be treated fairly and to know his place. He wants food, shelter, a place to come home to. Responsibility and to have his work appreciated. A dog wants to love and be loved. The same as people.

I got my character from my mother. She was the best mother a dog could have. There were seven of us in the litter. There wasn't a thing we did that she didn't get a laugh out of or didn't join in. Of course, we could be pretty annoying, too, but she nipped us if she had to. The anger came and went in a second. It's the hugging I remember, the hanging out together, the getting into that big, warm, sniffy ball of love. We all loved one another. It wasn't easy breaking up.

Anyway, here I was, and there was Gregory. Just a little kid then, pressed up against the wire, looking at me. It was a mutual thing. I was on my feet the minute I saw him, and got myself as close to him as I could get.

"That one," Gregory said, pointing to me.

"Good decision," his father said.

I know it's unwise to generalize about people, but you can tell a lot about a family by the way the kids act around their parents. And the other way around, too. I saw it there in the dog pound, that morning. Kids begging. Whining. Bored. Parents ignoring them. Families without character.

Gregory's father was different. He respected his son's judgment. "You picked the best dog in the place."

I don't go around inflating myself, but the truth was,

pound for pound, I probably *was* the best dog there. Not that I was physically impressive. I'm an average-size dog, maybe a little on the small side, but I can handle myself. I'm not talking about fighting ability. I'm talking about brains, and brains don't come by the pound.

Just as you can't generalize about people, you can't generalize about dogs. There are all kinds, all colors, all shapes and sizes. There are mean, scary dogs, but a lot more loyal, friendly, dependable dogs. Smiling, tail-wagging dogs. Play dogs. I-love-you-to-death dogs. Dogs that will go off with anyone. I'd advise keeping a dog like that on a leash. I hate a leash myself, but with some dogs you have no choice. I'm dog enough to say it.

2 ◎ The Oshuns opened their arms to me. They took me in, made me part of their family. They were Mom and Dad, and Gregory was my best friend. I got my ears pulled and my belly rubbed. At first they didn't know what to call me. I was part spaniel, so I had ears. Mom said my ears looked like big silk purse flaps, and she called me Silky Ears. Nobody else liked that name. Gregory called me Cosmos or Thunder.

"What an imagination," Dad said. "What a brain. You're a genius!"

"He's the genius." Gregory pointed to me.

"He does look a little like Einstein," Mom said, and they all went to look at the picture of Einstein that hung in Gregory's room. "He's got the same serious look, and look at the circles around the eyes."

From then on, I was Einstein. It was, "Einstein, where's Gregory? Einstein, don't let Gregory out of your sight." I didn't have to be reminded. Gregory was my boy and I was his dog. I prided myself on doing a good job. I never heard the words "bad dog," and I never was corrected, and I never ever heard anyone say, "What do you expect, he's only a dog."

You don't think that's humiliating? How would you feel if you heard, "What do you expect, he's only a human being?"

3 ◎ I consider myself a serious, one-person dog. That's the one person whose commands I take, the one person I want to be around. The one person I have to be with. Gregory. If he's not there, there's something missing in my life. I'm not scary-looking, like a Doberman or a bulldog, but if I think anyone is threatening Gregory, I can be ferocious. You don't put anything over on a really attentive, watchful dog.

Gregory was curious, always wanting to investigate things. If he saw a bee go into a hole, he'd get a stick and try to get it out. I'd bark to warn him, but he'd still get stung. He sniffed everything. Like me. He'd taste anything, even insects. Maybe he learned that from me, too. I like to snap at flying bugs.

He did have a way of getting into situations. He'd cross a busy street reading a comic. There were moments when all I could do was hold my breath. Like the time he climbed down a cliff over a busy highway. The cliff was so steep I couldn't follow him. I didn't know whether to wait on top and hope he'd make it, or run around to the bottom and block traffic in case he fell.

That's what I finally did, running out into a four-lane road. Oh, was I cursed and yelled at. "Crazy, stupid dog!"

Gregory came down fine. "Einstein," he said. "What are you doing down here?"

He was a dreamer. "Einstein," he said to me once, "what if we lived on another planet?" We were on the grass in the backyard. I was chewing on a bone I'd found in the bushes.

"I'll be an astronaut, and you be the first dog astronaut." He spread his arms and showed me the way we'd fly and land on a new planet. "I'll call it Smiggy. I'll be the first human to land there and you'll be the first dog. What are you going to say to the Smiggoids? Have you thought about it?"

I gave him a paw.

"That's right, you give them a paw and I give them a smile. You think they know what a smile means? To Smiggoids, a smile could be an insult." He pulled me around by my muzzle so I could see the smile he'd give the Smiggoids. "Guess what I'm saying now....Phew! You've got dog breath."

7

4 ◎ **After elementary school,** Gregory stopped playing astronaut and began noticing girls, and I began to hear a lot about one of them. Tina Sparks. How incredibly nice she was, how talented, and what incredible nerve she had.

"Einstein, remember Show Night? Tina got up in front of the whole school and sang and danced. Would you do that? I couldn't. I don't know where she gets the guts."

I liked Tina. She reminded me of a black poodle that used to live a couple of blocks down from us. That poodle had real class, but wasn't stuck-up. Tina was like that, and she liked Gregory. Everyone liked Gregory. He was nice to everyone, and he played the piano and got invited to a lot of parties.

I went to school with Gregory every day. I hated it when the bell rang and he went in, and I had to stay out. I tried to follow him in a few times and got chased. I'd go around the block and come back. I was always there waiting when Gregory came out of school. Once he hid me in his knapsack, and I went to class with him, until a teacher saw me peering out. We were both sent to the principal's office.

5 ◎ **Every morning I had to wake Gregory up.** It was my job to get him ready for school. Gregory was a deep sleeper. You could run over him and he'd go on sleeping. I jumped on the bed, barked, and sniffed around his neck. I loved the way he smelled in the morning. He tried to pull me down next to him. I squirmed free and dragged the covers off him.

If nothing else worked, there was one sure way to get him up: I licked the bottoms of his feet. He'd jerk his legs away and laugh himself awake.

When we went downstairs this particular morning,

Dad was sitting with his coffee and the newspaper. He had it folded to the sports page. "Adler got forty-four points last night," Dad said.

"He's good." Gregory went up for a couple of imaginary shots. "How's that, Dad?"

"That's the way. Think tall, Gregory. Friday night's the big game. Coach is going to be looking to you."

"Yeah, Dad."

Both of Gregory's older brothers had been outstanding basketball players in high school. Stars. Now Dad said it was Gregory's turn. "You've got a good shot from the outside, and you're smart and you know how to handle the ball. But you've got to go to the basket more."

"Yeah, Dad."

Gregory played in every game, but it was mainly to relieve the starters. Every time he went in, Dad was on his feet, cheering. He went to all the games.

"Gregory, you're at the cusp," he said. "Meaning you're at the edge of greatness. You just have to put it together. Look at your brothers." Dad got up and took his car keys from the counter. "You and your brothers, each one of you is a star."

"Yeah, Dad."

On the way to school Gregory was mumbling to himself. "Dad doesn't understand that I'm short. I'm *short*. I'm not tall like my brothers. I'm always going to be short. Okay?"

I didn't think short was bad. I was on the smallish side myself, but if I was on the team, it would be different for me than it is for Gregory. Four legs are better than two. Plus the leaping-ability factor. We canines can leap three or four times our height.

"I don't want Dad to come to the game Friday night, Einstein. He's got his hopes up too high. Stephens Academy is a big game. He's going to expect something *great* from me. I hate it when he gets that disappointed look. We have to figure out a way so he won't come."

Then he groaned because he knew there was no way Dad wouldn't be at the game.

6 ◎ **I smelled Ron Rathson before I saw him.** I could smell him a mile away. It was that disgusting cologne he used. He was particular about the way he dressed. There was always a crease in his jeans. He wore what all the boys wore, but he didn't look like anyone else, or smell like anyone else, either.

Ron Rat, that's what I called him. He was a smiling, smooth-faced, two-faced, stab-you-in-the-back rat.

He was in front of the school leaning against the wall by the steps. "Hey, Greg-o-ree," he said. He always had some mean trick up his sleeve.

"Hey, Ron," Gregory said.

"Hey, Greg-o-ree," Ernie Taylor joined in. He was Ron's sidekick, a beanpole with half a lemon for a brain.

Ron put his arm around Gregory and gave him a knuckle burn.

Gregory rubbed his head. "That hurts. Was that supposed to be friendly?"

Ron gave him a couple of rapid shots to the arm. All fun, except Gregory was always the one who ended up rubbing his sore arm or pinned to the ground.

Ernie leaned close to Gregory. "You want me to drown that ugly dog of yours?" he said.

"No thanks," Gregory said.

Another joke, but I knew better. Ernie was always trying to get me when Gregory wasn't looking. He liked to light matches and throw them at me. Once, I was outside school and he opened a door for me. Against my better judgment, I went in. I was looking for Gregory. But the minute I was inside, Ernie shut the outside door and left me trapped between two doors. The maintenance man found me in the morning.

When I came home, Gregory was a mess. He hadn't slept all night. He threw his arms around me. "Einstein, where were you? Why did you just go off that way and not tell me?"

I wanted to say it was Ernie. I was frustrated, and I started to howl. That's the only thing I don't like about being a dog—communication can be a problem.

"Let me drown that dog," Ernie said again. Once he got an idea in his head, he didn't stop. "I'll drown him in Swan Pond." The pond was behind the school on the other side of the playing field. When we were younger, Gregory and I used to chase the ducks around in the grass and make them fly up. "What do you say, Gregory? I'll take him off your hands."

Just then, Tina appeared. She was carrying an armful of

papers for a play she was directing called *The Day the School Burned Down*. Gregory held the papers while she adjusted the straps of her knapsack. He was always a little shy around Tina and looked at her shoes a lot. I sniffed them. Good smell there.

Ron smoothed his hair. He was so arrogant. "Hey, Tina, how's my girlfriend doing?"

"How many times do I have to tell you I'm not your girlfriend?" She took the papers from Gregory. "You going to try out for the play, Gregory? I need a school principal."

"I never acted," Gregory said shyly.

"I think you'd be perfect," Tina said.

Ron pounded Gregory on the head with a book and sent Gregory staggering. "He'd be perfect as the town drunk."

I backed up, growling.

"Oh, Gregory." Tina caught him and held him steady. "Are you all right?"

Ron grabbed me by the ears and flipped me over, but Gregory caught me before I hit the ground.

He held me in his arms. "I don't want you to do that again, Ron," he said.

I snarled at Ron. He smiled. "We were just playing around, weren't we, Einstein?"

7 ◎ **That night Gregory didn't sleep.** He kept talking to me. "Danny Russell wasn't at practice today, and Dreyfus looked dead on the court. He's sick; he can't keep his head up hardly. If Dreyfus can't play tomorrow, then it's me." He moaned. "What if I lose the game for us? Dad is going to be there. What am I going to do, Einstein?"

I tried to calm him down. I licked his arms. I lay on his chest and put my nose up against his cheek. That always worked. But not tonight.

"Poor Dad." He was panicking. "He's going to see me flub in front of the whole world. Everybody's going to be there. Maybe he'll get sick, Einstein, and he won't come. No, Dad never gets sick. Maybe *I'll* get sick. I'm sick now."

He started to shiver. He pulled the blankets around him. His teeth chattered, his voice shook. I lay close to him on the pillow. I wanted him to sleep, but his eyes kept popping open. "Einstein, I want to sleep and never wake up," he said.

8 ◎ I was running. Flat-out running, like nothing could ever stop me. A great, rolling, velvety feeling. The wind chilling my eyes, my ears flapping like banners.

I woke up, smelling bacon and coffee. It was morning and it was late. Light was coming in the window. I sat up and looked around for Gregory.

When I saw the other dog, I bared my teeth. I was the only dog allowed in this house. "Out! Out!" I barked.

My bark—there was something wrong with it. It was a hiccup, a burp of a bark. It wasn't my bark. It wasn't big and full, it didn't say, GET OUT OR I'LL TEAR YOUR HEAD OFF.

I lunged at the other dog. He knew he didn't belong

here. He lay on his back, tail tucked under him. I smelled submission. I saw terror in his eyes.

I stood over him. I was going to chew him to pieces. I looked down and saw my legs. My legs? Were those my legs? Those long, hairless, skinny things? Those pale sticks?

Someone had skinned me down to nothing.

There was something wrong with my back legs, too. Something wrong with all of me.

Then I saw Gregory—in the mirror. He was standing there, naked except for a dog collar around his neck. I barked at him to get going and get dressed. But when I turned around, I didn't see him.

That dog—the other dog—had climbed up on the chair. He was peering at me. There was something awfully familiar about him. About the eyes. They were Gregory's eyes. That was when I got scared, because I couldn't believe what I was thinking. I tried to dive under the bureau but I bashed my head. I was too big or the bureau was too small; I couldn't get under it the way I always did. Blood dripped from my head and fell on my paw. But there was no paw. When I looked, I saw a hand. I saw five separate fingers. I saw Gregory's hand.

The other dog started barking. A real dog's bark. *My* bark!

I fled under the bed and licked the blood from my fingers. They smelled like Gregory.

I lay there breathing hard. I examined my hand. I made the fingers wriggle. I made a fist and opened it. Gregory's fingers. Gregory's hand.

I was Gregory. I was me, Einstein, but I was in Gregory's body.

And that dog with Gregory's eyes? He was Gregory in my body.

He crept close to me. He put a paw on my arm and brought his nose close to mine, making sounds, the way I did when I wanted to tell Gregory something. I could almost hear him say, What do we do now, Einstein?

9 ◎ **"Gregory, will you please keep that dog quiet."** Mom opened the door. "Aren't you ready for school yet? What are you doing under the bed, honey? Stop playing and leave Einstein alone."

I waited until she closed the door, then I stood up. I wasn't used to being up this high, being up on my hind legs. I kept wanting to get down close to the floor and sniff around.

Gregory was acting crazy. He kept leaping into the air and barking and looking into my face. I finally got it. He was telling me to look at the clock. It was a school day.

"No, I'm not going." I didn't know exactly how it was happening, but I was speaking. My breath and tongue were doing it. There was a tickling in my mouth and words were coming out.

Gregory was in the closet, tugging at clothes. He brought me a shirt, then dragged a pair of jeans to me, and I put them on. Why were clothes invented, when skin and hair are so perfect? I couldn't feel the light or the air on my body. I hated the sneakers. It was like standing in boxes.

15

Mom and Dad were both in the kitchen. "You've got your shirt on backward, honey." Mom put down her cup of coffee.

I circled the room several times. I kept glancing at my empty dish in the corner.

Dad looked up. "Is that dog collar a new fashion?"

"I don't like it," Mom said. She ran her hand through my hair. "Your hair's a mess. Get me your brush."

I started to go back, but Gregory was ahead of me. He raced upstairs and returned with the hairbrush in his mouth.

"What a bright dog," Mom said.

"If you ever had any doubt," Dad said.

"I—he—Einstein understands everything," I said, adding, "he always did."

"Stop running around the room, Gregory," Dad said. "You're going to be late for school. Sit down, kiddo."

Gregory jumped up on my chair and put his paws on the table.

"Einstein," Mom said. "That's cute, but you don't belong here. Get down." She filled my food dish with kibble and put it down on the floor. "Over here, Einstein."

"I—he can stay at the table," I said. "He's part of the family, too, Mom."

She handed me a plate of eggs and potatoes, and while I was trying to figure out how to use the fork, Gregory got his nose into the plate and ate half of it. I pushed him aside. "My food," I growled.

Dad drove us to school. I had Gregory on my lap. I wasn't going to school without him. When Dad wanted to know why Einstein was in the car, I said this was "Bring Your Pet to School" day. Gregory sat and stared out the window, the way I used to. I always loved to ride in cars. He seemed to have the feeling of being a dog, but things weren't going as well for me. I had to resist the urge to stick my head out the window or lean over and lick Dad's face. I had to keep reminding myself that I was a boy now.

"Tonight's the night," Dad said. "You ready for the game?"

The game! "Uh, sure," I said. Everybody was going to think that it was Gregory on the team. Gregory on the floor playing. Only it was going to be me, Einstein, the dog. And what did I know about playing basketball? Was that something a serious dog was expected to do? Gregory, who had been so worried about playing, didn't look worried now. He was the dog and I was the boy. The game was my problem. I'd swear he was smiling.

10 ◎ **I put Gregory into the knapsack.** It was a squeeze, and he kept squirming and I told him to keep still. "I know it's tight in there, but I'm not going in that school alone. And don't poke your head out, either, or we'll both end up in the principal's office."

There were a couple of holes in the side of the knapsack where he could look out and nudge me one way or the other through the corridors.

I met Tina in the hall and stopped. "Hi, Tina."

"Ready for the big game tonight?" she said. She clapped her hands and did a couple of cheerleading moves, ending with a leap in the air. I'd never realized how cute and lively she was. Maybe it was being up this high that made me really appreciate her. Her hair smelled fantastic. I kept wanting to sniff it.

Gregory was wriggling in the knapsack. "Look," I said to Tina, and gave her a peek.

"Oh, Einstein, you're in school! You cute, clever little dog. You like it here?"

Ron Rat, in all his smelly cologne, came strolling over, smiling at Tina. I just got the knapsack closed in time. "Tina, you going to sit with me at the game tonight?" Ron said.

"I'm cheerleading," she said coolly. Then the first bell rang and she went off.

Ron turned to me. "How's our star basketball player?" He showed his teeth in what was supposed to be a smile. "All set to lose the game?"

"You're the one who knows how to do that, ratface."

His eyes opened and his ears turned red. He thought he was talking to Gregory who was always so polite. He went for me, but I was ready. I stepped aside and ducked into my classroom.

18

School was not easy. Now I appreciated what Gregory had to go through every day. Sit. Sit. Sit. Then sit some more. Listen to Mrs. Tannenbaum talk, talk, and talk. And then listen some more.

The knapsack was on the floor between my legs. Gregory kept squirming and turning and popping his head up, like he wanted to tell Mrs. Tannenbaum and everybody who he really was. But he couldn't tell anyone anything.

At least I could talk. I could see that it was easier for me, who never talked before, to be a boy, than for him, who talked all the time, to be a dog.

The girl next to me saw Gregory and laughed. "Look at the dog—," she began.

I put my hand over her mouth.

She shoved me away. "Mrs. Tannenbaum! Gregory put his smelly hand on me."

"We don't use our hands that way, Gregory," Mrs. Tannenbaum said. "Stand up and apologize."

"Sorry," I said, getting to my feet and stretching my arms. I still wasn't used to this body.

"Sorry? Is that all?" Mrs. Tannenbaum said. "I think you can say a few more words."

I shook my head. I couldn't think of anything else to say.

Mrs. Tannenbaum sighed. "I know you've got an important game on your mind, but I want you to remember, Gregory, school is important, too. All right, sit down."

I forgot how big I was and how much I weighed and how hard I could sit. Next thing I knew, I was on the floor and the seat was broken.

"Gregory!" Mrs. Tannenbaum said. "What a way to behave. I'm sorry that you're like this today." And then she sent me to the office.

In the principal's office I had to sit and wait for the second principal in charge of discipline. I had the knapsack next to me. Gregory peered at me reproachfully from under the flap. "Okay, I'm sorry about the seat," I whispered.

Every time the bell rang, kids looked in. "What happened, Oshun?" After a while, it seemed like everyone in school knew that Oshun was sitting in the office. Only now they were saying Oshun had gone berserk and punched Mrs. Tannenbaum, and was in the office, handcuffed to a radiator.

Gregory reached out and pawed me. "What?" I snapped. He kept pawing me. "What are you saying? You don't know the problems I'm having being you. You got it good."

He ducked down again then. I felt sorry. He was doing his best too. I sat with my hand in the knapsack, stroking his head. He was a good boy at heart. I mean, dog.

When I finally got in to see the second principal, she hardly said a word about the broken seat. All she wanted to know was if I was ready for the game tonight. "Yes, ma'am."

"Are we going to win?"

"Yes, ma'am."

She put her hand to her ear. "Are we going to win?"

"Yes, ma'am!" I barked.

"Now you're talking."

11 ◎ **At lunch, the woman behind the counter told**

me to stop sniffing the sandwiches. "Take what you want, and move on." I bought milk and sandwiches for Gregory and me. At the checkout I had a little trouble with the money so I threw it all down and got hollered at again.

Outside there were kids by the picnic tables and over by the pond. I saw Tina with some girls and near them, lurking, were Ron Rat and Ernie. I circled around the other side of the pond, by the edge of the woods, and let Gregory out of the knapsack. Poor Gregory! He was desperate to go. He made a dash for the bushes.

I got worried when he didn't come right back, and I started yelling, "Gregory! Here, boy!"

"Who are you calling Gregory, Gregory?" Tina said, coming over to me. She was sipping on her water bottle.

"Little Gregory," I said lamely.

"Who?"

"Him," I said as Gregory came out of the bushes.

"You call your dog by your name? That's unique!" She sipped from her water bottle. "Little Gregory and big Gregory. Who else would have thought of that?"

"Only sometimes," I said. "Here, Einstein!"

I unwrapped the sandwiches. "Einstein, which one do you want?"

"Can you tell which one he wants?" Tina said.

"Watch," I said. "Tuna? Cheese? Peanut butter?" I held each one up separately.

Gregory barked for the peanut butter and I gave him the sandwich.

Tina couldn't get over it. "He is the most brilliant dog."

"He's a mutt," Ron said, coming out from behind a tree.

"Who, Einstein?" Tina said. "He's no mutt."

"He's not the only mutt around." Ron gave me a big sneering smile.

The hair on the back of my head bristled. I sensed someone behind me, and I looked around and caught Ernie sneaking up on Gregory.

"No you don't!" I snatched up Gregory just in time.

"Come on, Tina," Ron said, "let's go for a walk in the woods. I want to show you the spring flowers."

"Yeah, flowers," Ernie leered. "Go for it, Tina."

"Shut up," Ron said, and kicked him in the butt.

Tina stroked Gregory's neck. "Imagine calling you a mutt. You're a brilliant scientist, aren't you, Einstein?" She kissed him on top of his head. Gregory looked soulfully at her. "You have the most beautiful eyes," she said, and gave him another kiss.

"She's kissing a dog," Ernie yelled. "Look at her, Ron."

Ron was a rat, but Ernie was a complete idiot.

12 ◎ There was team practice that afternoon. Gregory was on the sidelines and did his best to help me. I bounced the ball too hard at first and sent it flying up to the beams. Gregory barked at me sharply and ran out on the court and got yelled at. But then I got the hang of it, running with the ball and dribbling it. Maybe the moves were in my body—I mean, Gregory's body—because it wasn't that hard. But then dogs are naturally athletic.

Coach blew his whistle, and we started passing the ball. When I got it, I didn't want to give it up. I guess you could say my dog instincts took over. I took it to the basket. "Pass the ball, Oshun," Coach yelled.

My other weakness was my eyesight. Dogs can smell ten thousand different things, but they're not known for their great eyesight. I could see the hoop, but it was a little fuzzy, and at first my shots were either too short or too long.

"Stay with it," Coach said. "Don't lose your confidence."

The first time I sent the ball through the hoop, I got so excited I leaped up and barked, "Go! Go! Go!"

"Way to go! Keep it up, Oshun!" Coach yelled. He took me aside later and said, "You're doing great. I'm going to be looking to you for outside shooting tonight."

On the way home, Gregory ran ahead, then looked back and barked. He wanted me to hurry up. I was too slow for him. He was acting more like me, and I was acting more like him. At the house he got the ball from the garage and nosed it out into the driveway, where we had a basketball hoop set up. "I'm tired," I said, sounding just like him. "Coach wants me to rest up."

Gregory made me stay out there and shoot baskets. A set of ten from the foul line. "Okay?" I said. Gregory nosed the ball to another position, and I had to shoot ten more.

He was in charge, herding me around, barking at me.

When we finally went in, I collapsed on the rug in front of the TV and fell asleep. I didn't wake up till Mom and Dad came home. The TV was on and Gregory was lying against me with the remote under his paw.

"Look how relaxed that boy is," Dad said. "That's the mark of a big talent!"

"What's Einstein doing with the remote control?" Mom said.

I tweaked his ears. Gregory was surfing channels, the way he always did.

13 ◎ The gym was packed that night. The yellow and black Stephens Academy buses were lined up outside. They'd come out in force. Everyone from our school was there, too. It was standing room only. When our team came out on the court, a big cheer went up from our side of the gym. Tina was leading the cheers. Dad and Mom were sitting in the front row. Gregory was with them. Ron and Ernie were there, too, behind the team bench.

In the opening huddle, Coach said the Stephens team was taller and heavier, but we were more agile and faster. He wanted us to move the ball. "Don't let them trap you. Pass, pass, pass. Don't force the shots. If you see an opening, take a shot."

When the game started, I was on the bench. Dreyfus made a couple of quick outside baskets for us, and we went ahead. Those first scores sent a roar through the gym. Then Stephens evened things, and their side roared. When they went ahead, there wasn't a sound from our side. For a while they seemed to get every rebound and block every shot we attempted. But we came back and evened the score.

It went back and forth that way. Dreyfus began looking sick again, and Coach sent me in to give him a breather. All my outside shots missed. Gregory kept barking at me. Stephens tried to steal the ball out of my hands, but I hung on. I wouldn't let go. I ran with it and was called for walking.

"It's not a football, Oshun," Coach yelled. "Dribble the ball, bounce it, pass it!"

At the half we were down fourteen points. Dad came over. "I'm taking Einstein outside. You're doing great, son. You looked fabulous on the court."

"Thanks, Dad." I had to wonder about his eyesight. Maybe he'd been a dog once, too.

In the locker room, Coach gave us another pep talk. We had to take more shots. Pass the ball more. "You guys are standing around too much."

"Coach, I'm going to puke," Dreyfus said, and staggered to the bathroom.

"Well, Oshun." Coach looked at me, and he sighed. "Think you can get that practice magic back?" he said.

I didn't know what to say. There were no words.

When we went out for the second half, Gregory had crawled under the bench. I saw the whites of his eyes. *Do it for me,* his eyes said. *You've got to do it.*

Coach put me into the game.

"There goes the game, folks," Ron sneered. "Greg-o-ree is playing."

I did what Coach said. I passed the ball. Whenever I was open, I took the outside shot. The Stephens players kept jumping in my face, and I missed. I got jarred. I was tripped and fell a couple of times, but no fouls were called. Under the bench Gregory was curled up, shaking.

Stephens was up fifteen points. Coach pulled me out and put Dreyfus back in, but he couldn't do anything either. Stephens went up twenty points. Then twenty-five. Not a sound from our side of the gym. Then Dreyfus took an elbow in the midsection, and he went down and stayed down.

Coach sent me in again. There was nobody else. He didn't even tell me to do anything. The light had faded from his eyes. The game was lost. The Stephens team were high-fiving and grinning. I kept trying, but I couldn't make a basket. Each time I grabbed for the ball, it was somewhere else. The Stephens players were toying with me. I kept lunging for the ball and they kept throwing it over my head.

Somewhere in there, I stopped trying to play like a boy and started playing like a dog. I wanted the ball. I went for it. I went low. I went high. I scrambled. I got the ball. The first time I got it, I went for the basket, head down, dribbling, dodging, cutting one way and then the other. At the basket, I leaped up and dropped it in.

I did it again. I was low, so I went under one guy's arm and around two others, then leaped high. Again the ball went in. Their big guys blocked the basket. I kept leaping one way and then the other, the way a dog can leap, the way I leaped for the Frisbee when Gregory and I played. And the ball kept going in.

At first, we were so far behind nobody thought it mattered. Stephens had the ball. They were passing. I saw the ball in the air and snatched it like a Frisbee in flight. Before any of their players could catch me, I was down court and had another basket. Afterward, Dad told me, "That steal was the turning point of the game. When you made that basket the whole gym started screaming and it never stopped."

Gregory Oshun was the hero of the game. I mean I was, but it was "Gregory" they were screaming. We won by only a handful of points, but it was enough. "Gregory! Gregory!" My name, his name, our name was being called from all sides. Someone was taking pictures. I was hoisted up and carried around the gym. I saw Tina. I saw Dad and Mom. Gregory was smiling at me from the bench. Everyone was smiling at me.

14 ◎ When I came out of the locker room, the celebration was still going on in the parking lot. Mom and Dad were waiting by our car. "You're the star," Dad said. I got hugged and kissed again.

Tina was with her parents, but she ran over and hugged me. "I'm a friend of Gregory's," Tina said to Mom. "He's my best friend!"

"Well, then, come have ice cream with us to celebrate," Mom said.

"Where's that cute Einstein?" Tina said.

"I gave him to your friends to walk," Dad said to me. "They offered. They should be coming back right away."

"Friends?" I said. "Who?"

"There were two of them. One was tall and the other one—"

"That might be Ron and Ernie," Tina said.

"Nice boys!" Dad said.

Nice boys? He didn't know Ron and Ernie the way I did. Tina didn't either. Nobody did. I ran back to the school. The gym was empty. The custodians were sweeping with their big brooms. I went to the locker room. What if they'd stuffed Gregory into one of the lockers? "Gregory!" I yelled. "If you hear my voice, bark!"

"What'd you lose?" a custodian said.

"My dog. Have you seen him?"

"He's probably home looking for you."

I wanted it to be true, but I knew it wasn't. Gregory never took good care of himself.

Tina was waiting outside. "Did you find him, Gregory?"

I shook my head.

Tina went up on her toes trying to see out over the cars. "They could be anywhere, the woods or the pond. Don't look so worried, Gregory. I'm sure Einstein's fine."

"The pond!" I said. I took off running.

15 ◎ There was a small island in the middle of the pond and a narrow wooden walkway that crossed to it. That's where I found Ron and Ernie. They were holding a plastic bag.

When they saw me they swung the bag between them like a pendulum, up and back, then they flung it into the pond. I heard Gregory's panicked bark, and then a splash as the bag hit the water. Ron and Ernie high-fived.

I dove into the pond, went down, and felt along the bottom. It was all slime and mud. I came up with a handful of black gunk and branches. Tina shouted at me to go out farther.

I dove again and groped along the bottom. This time I found the bag and tore the plastic open with my teeth. Gregory was inside. He was limp. I grabbed him around the middle and brought him up to the surface. He coughed and struggled against me. We thrashed and went under again, down into the muck. We came up, still locked together. I clung to him. I held his hair in my teeth and pulled him to shore.

Tina waded out to us. "Oh, Gregory, that was so brave! And Einstein, you were brave, too! Poor thing!"

I ran up on the shore and shook myself dry. I was a dog again! Gregory sat on the bank, coughing and spitting up water and trying to pull on his clothes. "Gregory," I said, "Gregory, look at us!" But all I could do was bark.

16 ◎ Ron and Ernie were still on the walkway. I growled and showed my teeth. I leaped toward them. Gregory was a step behind me. One impulse seemed to grip both of us. It was as if my dog energy was still in him, and his boy energy was still in me. Ron and Ernie stared. Maybe they couldn't believe what they saw—a fighting mad Gregory and an avenging dog.

We hit them like two slam-dunking ballplayers, like a

couple of raging tacklers. Like a runaway steamroller. I hit them low and Gregory hit them high. We sent them spinning into the water like a couple of bowling pins.

"Help!" Ron yelled. He threw his arms around Ernie's neck. "I can't swim."

Ernie punched Ron and broke free. He swam to shore and ran off. Ron went under. He came up choking and crying. "I'm drowning. Help!" He went down again.

I would have let him drown. But Gregory ran to the island and came back with a branch that he held out to Ron. He clung to it, and Gregory and Tina pulled him to shore.

"Thank you for saving my life," Ron said. Then he looked at his shirt. It was filthy and torn. "My designer shirt!" There were tears in his eyes. "Do you know what this shirt cost me? Why did you throw me in the water, Oshun!" He looked down at his sneakers and moaned and held his head. Then he ran off.

17 ◎ **I know this is not an ordinary story,** but all I can say is that it happened to us. To me and Gregory. Maybe you'll believe me if I tell you how it ended.

Gregory returned to himself, but he was never quite the same. He told Dad that he wasn't going to play basketball anymore. He'd played because his brothers played and because Dad wanted him to. He'd never cared that much about it, and especially not now, with everyone expecting him to go on playing the way he had that night against Stephens.

It was hard for Gregory to disappoint Dad. "I want to tell Dad there are other things in life besides basketball. But what are they?"

I barked at him. I wanted to say that he'd find out soon enough. And he did. He got the lead in the musical Tina was directing. And he was good! The acting bug bit him. Not being so shy anymore, he discovered he loved getting up in front of an audience and hearing their applause.

Gregory wanted me with him more than ever. When he got the lead, he insisted Tina find a part for me.

"Can he sing?" Tina asked.

I had to audition. It was a little embarrassing. It wasn't my idea of the way a serious dog behaves. I did it for Gregory. For my audition, I sang three different notes. Tina spoke of them as musical howls. That's a matter of opinion. I made my debut as Sam the Singing Dog, who comes to the rescue when the fire alarm fails. I don't want to take anything away from Gregory, but I was the hit of the show.

Ron never stopped trying with Tina, and she never stopped saying no. When Gregory got the lead in the play, Ron demanded a leading part, too. He wanted to play the arsonist who sets the school on fire. Tina gave him the role of the caring school counselor, everybody's friend and advisor. The role must have rubbed off on him a little, because he mostly stopped harassing Gregory.

Gregory never talked to anyone about what happened to us. Who would have believed it? He kept talking about it to me. Of course, I listened. I've always been Gregory's perfect listener.

Gregory and I have walked in each other's shoes—or as I like to say, paws—and it changed us forever. Gregory said what happened to us changed his life. That his eyes were open now. You had to go for what you believed in. Not to be immodest, but I always thought that, in that turnaround, some of my outlook on life rubbed off on him, and stuck.

"If I could only figure out how it happened, Einstein...," he would say time after time. "It's like a dream, isn't it, Einstein? Is it that way for you, too?"

For me? No. For me it was all real. Things happen, and then more things happen, and there's no use trying to figure them out, because you never will. That's the way I see it.

PUPPY LOVE

A PRISONER IN CLIFFSIDE PARK

Newark International Airport was a huge place. Coming off the plane, while I was still in the tunnel, I suddenly panicked. What did my uncle look like? What if he wasn't here?

"Jerry looks like your dad," Mom had said, "and so do you."

The trouble was I couldn't remember what my father looked like. He had died when I was a baby.

There was someone waiting at the gate. His fist shot up in the air when he saw me. He was in whites: T-shirt, pants, and sneakers. A tennis player, maybe. A movie star?

A chain-saw murderer? Or just a guy who liked to come to the airport in white clothes and meet people? His hair was a little thin on top, but he had a nice braid in back. Was that my uncle? He had a maniac smile and a voice you could hear from one end of the airport to the other. "Lucas?" he boomed.

I had my camera around my neck, but I didn't take a picture. There was still doubt in my heart. "Uncle Jerry?" I said.

"Uncle?" He looked around. "Who that? So you're Lucas. Hey, you're big. You look terrific." And then he grabbed me, got his arm around my neck. I thought he was going to choke me. I fought free.

"Hey, what's the matter?" he said. "I just wanted to give you a little hug. You know, men can hug and kiss now."

I wanted to get back on the plane. Nothing personal, but I wanted to go home.

"Let me get that," he said, trying to take my knapsack.

"It's okay, I've got it."

"It looks heavy."

"It's light." The knapsack weighed a ton. I'd packed it with magazines and books I was going to read this summer.

"Lucas! Do I call you Lucas, or do you prefer *Sir* Lucas?" He laughed like he'd said something really witty.

"Lucas is okay, Uncle Jerry."

"Call me Jerry," he said. "'Uncle' is for old guys." He had very large bright blue eyes.

It was hot on the highway. I knew I wasn't going to

find my father here. I wasn't looking for my father. But I must have expected something, because I felt let down. I kept striking my cigarette lighter. It was just something I did with my hands, but Jerry acted like I had a nicotine habit ten miles wide. "I don't want you smoking in my car or my house or anywhere near me."

"I don't smoke," I said.

He kept going. It was bad for his health, he said, bad for my health. He didn't like smoking, his girlfriend, Kiki, didn't smoke, and he didn't want me smoking. "I'd hate to have to tell your mother I'm sending her back a tobacco junkie."

At that point I was tempted to jump out and hitchhike back home.

Coming here had been Mom's idea. She was going to summer school in Pittsburgh to get a year's worth of credit in speech therapy, and I was going to Cliffside Park to bond with my uncle. Translation: I'd be in a safe place, and she wouldn't have to worry about me every minute.

"No arguments, Lucas," she'd said. "End of discussion. Period."

"Who's arguing, Mom?" I'd said, wanting to argue. "I'll go to Pittsburgh with you."

"And live with me and three other women in one room?"

"Then I'll stay home."

"No way am I leaving you alone for six weeks."

What Mom thought was her winning argument was that I was going to spend time with my uncle Jerry, my father's brother. "Your closest male blood relation."

I didn't know about the blood, but like so much stuff in my life it was a done deal. If Mom had had to, she would have packed me in a box and shipped me to Jerry UPS. I couldn't wait to grow up and be on my own.

Jerry drove and talked. And talked. He talked about himself, his running, his biking, his business. He repaired rips, tears, and burns to automobile upholstery. "All the damage people do to the inside of their cars. Cigarette burns—they're the worst. I use a secret formula." He lowered his voice. "I can't even tell you, Lucas."

"That's okay," I said.

After the highway, we drove down long avenues, past street after street of little houses. "Here we are," Jerry said, pulling into a driveway. He jumped out of the car and yelled to a man in the yard next door. "Hey, Dave." The man was holding a long pole with a pair of shears at the end of it, and he was cutting branches. "This is my nephew, Lucas," Jerry called.

The man leaned the pole against a tree and walked back to his house.

"He doesn't like me," Jerry said. "I talk to him every time I see him and he's never answered me." He smiled like it was the greatest thing. "He hasn't talked to me in five years. What do you think of that?"

Any thought that Jerry was like my father went out the window. I went back to the theory that he was a maniac.

In the kitchen he said, "Sit down, Lucas. I bet you're starved."

I didn't sit down. "I'm here under duress," I said.

"Du ress?" he repeated, and gave me that weird grin.

"Duress means I don't want to be here."

"I know what duress means, Lucas. Don't worry, you'll get used to it. You're not going to run away, are you?"

"No. I'm not going to run away."

"Good. I'd hate to call your mother and say I don't know where you are."

"Nobody has to watch me," I said. It sounded babyish. Everything I said sounded stupid here.

Later he showed me my room. "You're going to love it," he said. It was half the size of my room at home. It had a bureau and a cotton mattress rolled up against the wall. He got me sheets, a pillow, and towels, and he brought in a framed picture of him and my father when they were boys. "Did you ever see this? You can tell we're brothers, can't you?" He set the picture on the bureau. How's that? Something to think about, isn't it? Well, good night. I probably won't see you in the morning."

I opened the window. I rolled out the mattress. It was too hot for blankets. I kicked my sneakers off, threw off everything but my shorts, and lay down. I thought of my room, the posters on the walls, the model cars in the bookcase. My computer! Mom's friend had found it for me secondhand. I could find things to do in my room at home for weeks.

This room was like a cell in a prison. I was the prisoner and Jerry was the warden. Mom was the parole board. I wasn't getting off till I served my sentence.

RUNNING GIRL

The first time I saw Running Girl I was sitting on the steps of Jerry's house, fingering the cigarette lighter and watching the leaves tipping and bobbing in the light. It was too hot to be inside.

It was my third day. Jerry wasn't around much. He had his job, his daily workouts, his girlfriend. That morning, while it was still cool, I'd walked around the neighborhood. I had found the library, an ice-cream shop, a diner. I went in and ordered blueberry waffles with the money Jerry had left me. I bought myself a comic and went back to the house and read it. I thought about Billy, Howard, and Trac. I imagined the three of them sitting at the edge of the swimming pool at Schiller Park, maybe talking about me and thinking I was in New York City this very minute, up on top of the World Trade Center. I'd told them my uncle and I would be doing all this great stuff. I didn't tell them I was going to be stuck in Cliffside Park, across the river from New York, all summer.

I struck the lighter too hard and it flew out of my hand. That's when Running Girl and her pack of dogs appeared. She was about my size, big, and a little overweight, like me. Long hair down to her waist, a flash of earrings. Older. Her legs were going up and down, they were rotating, they were moving forward.

I didn't know why I was looking at her. I wasn't interested in girls. Trac would tell you that. Howard was interested, but he was peculiar anyway. He had a mustache already, or what he called a mustache.

It wasn't like she was the first girl I'd ever seen, either, but I got up and followed her. I couldn't help myself. If Trac were here, he'd say I'd lost my brains. By the time I got to the corner, I was sweating and she was out of sight. "Jerk," I said to myself, "running after a girl you don't even know."

It was all part of this moron summer. Living with my uncle, who I hardly knew, in a place I didn't want to be. I sat outside and waited for Running Girl and the dogs to come by again.

I WAVE TO RUNNING GIRL

Whenever I saw Running Girl, she always had dogs with her. Three red dogs one day, then a fat white one and a bunch of brown dogs the next. The day after that they were all beagles. Maybe she loved dogs so much she went around begging people to let her run their dogs. Or she had a dog-sitting service. Or she worked for a dog kennel. I began to wish I had a dog so we could meet. People with dogs always talked.

One day, I waved, and she waved back. I wanted to talk to her, but she went by too fast and I was too lazy—too slow to get up and follow her. But mostly, I was too shy.

THE MORE YOU DO,
THE MORE YOU DO

"Meet Moose the Noose." Jerry ripped off his tie and held it out like something dead. "I hate this thing."

"Why do you wear it?"

"It's my badge. I'm a professional, an engineer of auto beautification. Without it, I'm just a grease monkey. I had a fantastic day today. How was your day?"

"Okay."

"Just okay? I want you to have a really terrific time." He got me in an armlock. "I mean, really. You having fun here? I worry about you. You don't talk much, do you, Lucus? Are you happy? I want you to be happy. It'll make me happy. Do you know what I'm saying? It's not like we're strangers. I mean, me and your father, you and me, it's blood. That's heavy, man."

He rapped his head into mine and for a minute we stood that way, squeezed tight against each other, our heads together like we were both thinking deep into each other's minds.

The phone ringing broke the spell. He went to take his messages off the machine. I could hear them echoing from the other room. One hollow voice after another. Most of them were about work.

Because Jerry got mostly business calls, I wasn't supposed to answer the phone when he wasn't there. If he wanted to talk to me, he said, he'd ring twice and hang up. "Then I'll ring three times and hang up. That'll be the signal. Then the next time I ring, you pick up. Is that brilliant, or is that brilliant?"

"Brilliant," I said.

"How many push-ups can you do, Lucas?"

"I don't know."

42

"I could do a hundred at your age." When he wasn't working, he was running or biking or in the gym. He was training for a triathalon—an eighteen-mile run, a five-mile swim, and a twenty-two-mile bike race. "Can you do ten push-ups?" he asked.

"I guess so." In school, I mostly faked them. The gym class was big and the teacher couldn't see everyone.

"Come on, let's do some together."

I got down and did ten and stopped.

"Let's have another five," Jerry said. He was doing them with me, but on the tips of his fingers.

I did five more.

"Super, Lucas! Each day, add another five. Before you know it, you'll be ripping off a hundred like it's nothing. The more you do, the more you do. That's a life lesson, Lucas."

I'd made him happy.

RULES FOR DOGS

Every day I thought about talking to Running Girl. In my head I had these fantastic conversations with her, where I'd talk and she'd listen, and everything I said was incredible.

By accident one morning, I saw her going into McKessney Park. There was a bagel shop near the entrance where I sometimes stopped, and I saw her going into the park with a German shepherd. I followed her and watched as she and the dog ran around the track.

There was a playground nearby. I watched the kids

playing basketball, and I watched her. After she finished running, she went into the bagel shop. The shepherd sat outside—no leash, not even tied up. He just sat there and waited. Inside, Running Girl was standing in line. I got up close to her; I was almost next to her, but she didn't recognize me. I was like a shadow she didn't know she had.

After that, I hung around in the park so much that the basketball players started asking me to play whenever they needed somebody. I played, but not as good as I could have, because I always had an eye out for Running Girl.

I imagined the different ways I could introduce myself to her. I'd be walking by one day, looking good, my hair combed, just passing by, sort of loose and light. She'd have a dog with her. I'd probably have a dog, too.

—That's a nice dog you've got there. What's his name?

—Dog, I'd say.

—Doug?

—Yeah, Doug, I'd say.

And a nice conversation would ensue.

Late one afternoon, I was hanging out with the basketball players and I saw her sitting by herself on a bench near the track. She just had the one dog with her, the German shepherd, who was sniffing around the grass.

44

I borrowed a pack of cigarettes from one of the kids. Just having it in my pocket gave me the nerve to walk over to her. When I got near, I lit one. "Hi." I held the cigarette up. "What's your name?"

She sort of half looked at me and didn't answer.

Okay, she didn't like me. She was too old. I was too young. Whatever.

She brushed the air. "Why do you want to know my name?"

"Because."

"Because?"

"Because I want to talk to you."

"My name is Glori."

"I never knew a girl with that name. Glori. It's a name I'll never forget."

"Really? What's your name?"

"Lucas."

"Lucas," she repeated. "It's a name I'll never forget."

I sat down near her, holding the cigarette away from her. "You want one of these?"

"I don't smoke, Lucas."

"I don't either."

She looked at me.

"Except sometimes, when I'm nervous."

"What are you nervous about?"

"You," I said. "I never talk to girls."

"I guess now you do."

"I guess so."

I couldn't believe it. We were talking. Then I couldn't think of what to say next. I guess she couldn't, either, because we just sat there.

"I see you with dogs all the time," I finally said. "Are they all yours?"

"Lucas, are you kidding? It's a job. One of several." She

showed me a bunch of keys on her belt. "People go to work, I go to their house, I get their dog, I exercise it, I bring it home, I feed it. They pay me."

"They must trust you."

"Would you? Do I look trustworthy?"

"You do to me."

"You don't know me."

"I'd trust you with anything," I said.

"Give me some money."

I had a couple of bills, and I gave them to her.

"Say good-bye to your money," she said.

"I don't care," I said. "Keep it. I'll bring you some more tomorrow."

"Now I know we're friends," she said, and handed the money back to me. She called the dog. "Belle!" The shepherd's ears perked up, and she came over. Glori hugged her.

"This sweet girl here is mine. Aren't you, Belle? You have a dog, Lucas?"

"My mother says it would be unfair to any animal to have to live with me."

Glori looked me over. "You don't look that bad to me, Lucas. What's the real reason? Your mom afraid of dogs?"

"No, the rule of the house we live in says no dogs."

"You've missed a lot." She brushed away the smoke. "Why don't you put that smelly thing out, Lucas?"

I carefully stubbed out the cigarette and put it back in the pack. "I get to meet dogs," I said. "I've just met Belle. She's friendly."

"Sure, when she's with me. There are a lot of un-trained, undisciplined, unpredictable dogs out there. Not Belle! I run a training class for dogs in the park three days a week, and I know if anybody does."

"That another job you have?"

"You are right. I'm one hardworking woman."

"If I had a dog, I'd put her in your training class. Not that my dog would need it. I have a few rules of my own for dogs, and I've never been bitten or anything close."

"Such as?" she said.

"Rule one, always stop and talk to any dog you meet. Rule two, never run from a barking dog. Rule three, always smile at dogs."

"Sounds good to me. There's a little more to it, of course." She got up to go. "Come on, Belle, we have to get going. See you around, Lucas."

I sat there thinking about the fantastic conversation I'd just had. Then I went and gave the kid back his cigarettes.

MY UNCLE TELLS ME ABOUT GIRLS

Jerry never cooked. We had takeout a lot and some-times we went to a pizza house and shared what Jerry called "a big one." He insisted I have salad, too. "I'm not a salad man," I said. He kept pointing to things I should add to the salad. When we sat down, he said, "Just two guys having a good time."

"Did you and my father do this?" Every night I looked at the picture of him and my father. A tall blond boy with his arm around a short blond boy. They looked like brothers.

He broke a piece from the pizza. "Your father was older. He had his own friends. But he was one great guy. One great brother. Everyone liked him." Jerry's eyes got a little damp.

I knew that look. When I asked anything about Dad, Mom got it, too.

"You miss your dad?" Jerry asked.

"Sure," I said. "But you can't miss too much what you've never had." It was what I always said, like I didn't care. I didn't want people feeling sorry for me.

"I bet it's hard on you, guy. No father." His eyes got that sticky red look again. "I wish he was sitting here with us right now."

"Do you know what I did today?" I said to change the subject. "I talked to a girl in the park."

"What girls?"

I held up one finger. "Girl."

"Ooh! You saw a girl, you liked her, you talked to her. And now you've got a girlfriend! Hey, that's good, man. Good work."

"She's not a girlfriend."

"Yes she is. Yes she is!" He was grinning at me. "What's her name?"

"Glori."

"Great! That's a great name. How old is she?"

"I don't know."

"Where does she live?"

"I don't know."

"You didn't ask her? You're shy? You want me to talk to her for you?"

"No."

"You're right, I better not. Girls go nuts over me. I'd steal her away from you." He looked really happy again.

"She only talks to dogs," I said.

KIKI COMES TO BREAKFAST

Saturday morning, when I went into the kitchen, Kiki, Jerry's girlfriend, was there. I'd never met her, but I knew it was her. She was built like Jerry, tall, blond, and lanky. She even wore the same style green and white sweats. There was a bank-sponsored ten-mile run that morning starting at the reservoir, and they were both in it.

"Hi, Lucas, I'm Kiki."

"I know."

"Jerry said you're a terrific kid. I bet you are! Listen, Lucas, will you tell the big guy to hurry up?"

"Jerry," I called. "Hurry up."

"What do you want for breakfast?" Kiki said. "We don't eat much the morning of a race. I'm going to have a piece of toast and jam. You can have French toast, if you want to."

"Okay." I got the bread and eggs from the refrigerator and started the pan heating.

Kiki broke two eggs into a shallow bowl. "How's your summer going, Lucas? You accomplishing a lot?"

"I can do twenty push-ups now."

"That is incredible! Way to go, Lucas."

She *sounded* like Jerry, too.

When he came down, he gave her a long kiss on the mouth. "That's the way I like to start every day," he said.

"Stop," Kiki said. "You're going to embarrass Lucas." She served me the French toast.

Jerry sat down with a banana and a glass of water. "I'm going to ace this race," he said. "You heard me say it. I'm going to win. You're both going to be there cheering me on."

"Hey, I'm running too," Kiki said. "Remember?" She spread some jam on her toast. "So the only way I'm going to be cheering you, Jerry, is if I break a leg."

Jerry winked at me. "Okay. Lucas is going to have to do it for both of us, then."

THE INCREDIBLE OFFER

Kiki came in third in the women's division, but Jerry won the men's, just the way he'd predicted. Afterward, he couldn't stop talking about it. "I told you guys," he kept saying on the way home. "I told you guys I would." He banged on the steering wheel. "Was that incredible, or what?"

"Incredible," Kiki, who was sitting next to him, agreed.

"I ran an incredible race!"

"Incredible."

"How about Kiki's race?" I said. I was behind them. "She ran a good race, too."

Kiki turned and gave me a thumbs up.

"Incredible," I said again. I kept thinking about Glori. Would she remember me when she saw me again? Maybe I'd have to remind her. *Hey, Glori, it's me! Lucas, the boy without a dog.*

"How you doing, Lucas?" Jerry glanced back at me. "Lucas, was I great or was I great?"

"You were great," I said. "And Kiki was incredible!"

"You're right, man. I want you to have a great day, too. What can I get you, Lucas, to make this a great day for you?"

"Lucas, make it good," Kiki said. "He won't make an offer like this again for another ten years."

"Anything, Lucas," Jerry said. "Come on, man. Name it, old son."

"A dog," I said, not meaning it at all, just thinking of Glori and saying it. She'd like it if I had a dog.

MICHAEL

"You ask Jerry for something, you get it," Jerry said.

It was Monday, and Jerry had just come home from work, and yes, he had a dog in his arms, and it was all he could do to hold it.

"What's that?" I said stupidly.

"Your dog."

"I don't want a dog," I said.

"Sure you do. That's what you told me. I got her from a customer. I said, 'Peter, I'm looking for a dog.' And he said he had one for me. Just like that. He's a busy guy. His daughter left the dog with him, and he's got no time for it. I said, 'Give it to me, I have the right person for her.' Watch this, Lucas."

He put the dog down. She was an all-brown, short-haired dog. "This is one smart dog. Sit, girl," he commanded. The dog leaped into the air. She went up like a rubber ball. Long legs, big, upright ears. She looked like a little deer.

"Sit! Sit, girl!" Every time he said sit, she sprang.

"Maybe English is her second language," I said.

"She's yours," Jerry said.

"What am I going to do with her? I don't know anything about dogs."

"You're going to do great, Lucas. Sit, girl; come on, sit," he pleaded, but the dog kept leaping.

"What's her name, Michael Jordan?"

"Michael! Great name. Is that what you're going to call her?" Jerry put the leash on her, then handed it to me. "Dogs and boys, Lucas. Like ducks and water." He went into the house.

Michael and I looked at each other. She was beautiful, but I was scared of her. Not scared that she'd bite me. Just scared.

"Dog," I said. "Sit." She sprang. She was all over me, trying to lick my face. "Sit," I yelled. "Sit, Michael!" She didn't pay any more attention to me than she had to Jerry.

I got her into the house. I didn't want to drag her, and she didn't want to go in, so it took me a while. In the kitchen, she stepped in the water bowl and sent water

52

splashing over the floor. Then she lapped it up like she'd just spent six months in the desert.

She got into everything, sniffed in every corner, ate everything I put down for her. She didn't know what halfway meant. She ate a can of dog food in seconds, scarfed it up, then pushed the bowl around with her nose until I filled it again. Then she got her paws up on the table, looking for more.

"Hungry little beggar," Jerry said. "Knock her paws off the table, Lucas."

I wasn't knocking her off anything. I got my arms around her and set her down. Jerry said I should keep her in the garage, but I'd already decided that she was going to sleep in my room.

It was nice having her there. We played, but when it was time to go to sleep, she didn't like the special place I'd made for her near my bed. She got on the mattress with me, curled up in back of my knees, and went to sleep.

In the middle of the night I woke up and heard her sniffing around the room. I'd put some papers down and she peed on them.

Jerry was right about one thing—she was smart. "Good girl," I said. She licked my face with her rough, wet tongue. "Hey, Michael. Cut it out."

She dashed around, barked, and wanted to play. Every time I fell asleep she did something and woke me up. In the morning I could hardly get my eyes open.

• • •

I was going to go to McKessney Park and show Glori the dog, but I never got there. Michael ran me all over the place. I spent all morning feeding her, cleaning up after her, chasing after her. I barely got her out of the house to do her business. She did it on the neighbor's lawn, the grumpy one, the one with the shears, the one who never talked to Jerry.

He talked to me, though. He saw the whole thing. "Clean up that mess," he said. "And take it all home with you."

That night, Jerry brought home Chinese takeout. I shared my fried rice with Michael. She was crazy for it. She cleaned out the carton. She ate more than I did.

"You're starting a bad habit," Jerry said. "She's going to beg for table food all the time now. Give her dog food."

"I don't like dog food."

"I'm not asking you to eat it, Lucas."

She went over and got her nose in Jerry's dish. "Who invited you?" Jerry said, pushing her away.

"Don't be mean, Jerry. She's young, she's growing, she needs a lot of food."

"Not mine," Jerry said. "Go on, you garbage can, get away."

"Don't call her that." I wrapped my arms around her. "Her name is Michael." She was warm and smooth, and I could feel the thick muscles under her coat. She kept looking around at me with those big goofy deer eyes like, *What do we do next, Lucas?*

MICHAEL ENROLLS IN SCHOOL

"Look, Michael, I want to impress my friend Glori by training you, and you're not cooperating. Sit!" I said.

She jumped.

When I said come, she yawned.

When I said heel, she lay on her back for me to scratch her belly. It was all a game to her.

"Michael, no scratching, no playing, no getting your ears stroked till you listen." I snapped my fingers. "This means come. Okay? You got it?" I snapped my fingers.

She wandered off to investigate a piece of paper in the corner of the room.

I grabbed her and held her down. "You have to sit when I tell you to sit. Sit!"

She wriggled out from under my hand and barked, like this was a really good game.

"Okay. I give up."

Glori held her dog obedience class in the afternoon. I didn't know which afternoon, but I found out by going to McKessney Park. I was lucky. The very first time Michael and I went there, a faded red pickup truck drove up, and Glori was in the passenger seat. Her dog was in back and a guy with a shaved head was behind the wheel.

"Michael," I whispered, "now we do it. We're going to make a great impression on Glori. When I say come, you—"

Just then Michael spotted Belle, Glori's shepherd, and

like a shot she was off. She threw herself at Belle, sniffing around the way dogs do.

"Is this your dog?" Glori said. "Call her off."

"Michael, come here. Michael!"

I had to run after her, but that wasn't the worst of it. When I picked her up, she nipped at me. "Hey!" I slapped her on the muzzle.

"She shouldn't be biting," Glori said. "And you shouldn't be hitting her."

"I wasn't. And she doesn't," I said quickly.

"She needs to be trained." Glori was frowning. "An untrained dog is an unmanageable dog."

"She's my first dog," I said.

"I know. I know."

So she did remember me. "I want to enroll her in the class."

"Give me a paw," she ordered, and took Michael's paw in her hand. "Let's see if she's going to cooperate. Shake, girl." She moved Michael's paw up and down. "That's the way, girl." She tickled Michael's ears and did it again. "Shake."

The paw went up and down, then the petting and the praise, then the paw again.

"She's doing it!" I said. "She's shaking."

"Of course she is. She's going to do really well. Shake," she said, and Michael put out her paw.

I stuck out my paw, too.

"Oh, you're a couple of cute pups," Glori said.

PROFESSOR GLORI

Glori was a great teacher. Even after one class, Michael behaved better. She actually came when I called her and sat when I told her to sit. Jerry thought the training class was a brilliant idea. "You really showed initative there, Lucas. I'm proud of you. Things are shaping up for you now."

There were three women and another boy around my age in the first class, but the boy never showed up again.

The guy in the red pickup always dropped Glori and Belle off. Sometimes he hung around. Sometimes he left and came back later. I didn't like him. I was always glad when he left.

At the start of each class, Glori would give a little lecture. "Dogs are pack animals, like wolves. There's the top dog, the alpha dog. It's like a ladder and on the next rung down there's an underdog, and a dog under that dog. And so on. Dogs want to know their place. Since most dogs don't live in packs, but with their owners, you have to be the top dog. Even if it's only one dog, you're the leader of the pack. Don't ever forget that."

During class, Glori gave each dog a lot of attention. "People, I want you to hug your dog every day. Talk to your dog. Get down there on all fours, on your dog's level, and hug him and show him how much you love him. Lucas, demonstrate how you love Michael."

"Yes, Professor Glori." I wound my arms around Michael's chest and hugged her.

"Look how happy Michael looks," Glori said. "Aren't you, Michael?"

Glori was nice to everyone, but I thought she was extra nice to Michael. And to me, too.

I never missed a class. I came early, so I could talk to Glori before the others arrived. I brought bagels to share with her. I took pictures of the class with my camera and gave them to her. On one I wrote "For Professor Glori." I didn't tell her I liked her, but I think she knew. When class was over, and if her boyfriend wasn't back, I'd hang around and talk to her some more. It was a lot about dogs, but other things, too. I found out she was in college, and that the guy in the red pickup *was* her boyfriend, and his name was George.

One day he stayed and ate all the bagels. I had four of them in the bag and he didn't even say thanks. I didn't like anything about him. Not his name. Or his sleeveless sweatshirts. Or the rings he wore on his fingers or the chains around his neck.

Glori showed me a silver ring he'd given her. It was in the shape of a snake with ruby eyes. It was too big for her, and she wore it on her thumb. George had a lawn-mowing business. She'd worked with him at the beginning of the summer until she got the job running dogs.

"You're better off without him," I said.

"Why? Don't you like him?"

"He thinks he's so big."

"Oh, you're just too young to understand some things." And then she lectured me. "When you tear someone down, it's a sign of weakness, not strength, Lucas. You need to learn to look beneath the surface, to understand a person's true character. When you get older, you'll see."

"He loves himself too much," I said. "That pearl in his ear. What's that for?"

"He's different. He's not like everyone else."

"He's an alpha dog."

Glori laughed. She pulled my ear. "Are you jealous, Lucas? I can be friends with more than one person."

One day Michael and I walked her and Belle home. There was a wire fence around her house and two more dogs in the yard: A miniature collie that belonged to her sister and Boy, her mother's old black Labrador. The dogs came to greet Glori, but they were really excited about Michael.

We watched the dogs playing for a while. Glori started asking me a bunch of questions, about my father and my uncle and why I was in Cliffside Park this summer.

"Is Jerry like a father to you?"

"No," I said.

"Why not?"

"He's just not."

"What does that mean? Be more specific."

"I don't know. He's okay."

"Okay? Does he like you?"

"I guess so. I'm in his house. He invited me to come."

"And do you like being there?"

I got down with Boy and scratched him under the chin. "You really know how to ask questions," I said.

"I should. Journalism is my second choice if I don't get into medical school—"

"So I'm your guinea pig?"

"That's right." She tapped me on the head. "Sure you are."

I wanted to tap her back, but I didn't know if I should. I liked her touching me. I wished she'd do it some more.

THE GIRL IN THE BAGGY SHORTS

One day there was another girl in the truck with Glori and George. They all got out and stood there talking. The other girl wore work boots and a shirt so short it showed her belly button. After a while she and George drove off together.

"Do you like Esther?" Glori asked me after the class. I was holding a pocket mirror up for her while she pinned her hair back.

"She's okay," I said. "Cute belly button."

"Cute, nothing!" Glori grabbed the mirror back from me. "That's really stupid, Lucas. You guys!"

"Glori, I didn't mean—"

"Oh, I know what you meant."

"Glori, I—"

"No! I don't want to hear anything else. Good-bye, Lucas."

I sat down under a tree. Michael went sniffing around. I was supposed to work her, practice the lesson. Send her out and call her back. Walk and make her heel and sit. I didn't do any of it. "Michael. Here!" She came right over.

I got my arm around her. "You think Glori's really mad at me? Maybe she won't want us in the class. You think?"

Michael barked. She had developed this goofy way of barking, halfway between a whine and a bark, that was like talk. Maybe nobody else understood, but I knew what she meant. *Cool it. It's going to be all right, Lucas. Come on, let's play!*

Esther, the other girl, was there again on Thursday and hung around with George while Glori ran the class. For a while they sat on the hood of the truck. He had his head in her lap, and she was smoothing his eyebrows. Glori kept looking over at them.

Then Esther slid off the truck and George chased her around. She jumped into the cab and blew the horn.

"Will you guys cut that out," Glori yelled. "Just stop!"

George froze, like he was playing statues. Esther was smiling at him from inside the cab.

"There's a class going on," Glori said. She looked upset. She ended the lesson ten minutes early, and they all drove off together.

"I hate him," I told Michael. "What a pig. How many girlfriends does he need?" I wanted to do something for Glori. Something great. Maybe I'd die for her. No, I didn't want to die, but I wanted her to know I would if I had to.

61

WHAT HAPPENED IN THE BAGEL SHOP

I saw Glori at the bagel shop, sitting by herself in a corner. She looked sad, but when she saw me she waved me over. "Hi, Lucas. Where's Michael?"

"I left her home." I sat down and offered her part of my bagel. "Nice and hot," I said.

She shook her head. "Nothing for me. So, how're you, Lucas?"

I started blabbing about Michael and how this summer had turned from bad to brilliant, all thanks to Michael. "And you," I said.

"Me? That's nice." She played with the silver ring George had given her. "How're things going with your uncle?"

"Good. Jerry does his thing, and I do mine."

"Your uncle should be more like a father to you, a role model. That's what your mother wanted. That's why she sent you here. He should be thinking about you more. He's selfish. All he thinks about is himself."

"He got me Michael."

"He got you a dog, but where's he? Does he really care about you? All guys think about is themselves."

"Jerry's okay," I said. Why was she acting so upset about him? She didn't even know him.

"You've got a right to be disappointed, Lucas. I know what it's like to be disappointed in someone." Tears ran down her cheeks.

I didn't know what to do. I handed her a napkin. "Did I do something wrong, Glori? Are you mad at me?"

She wiped her face. "Not you. You're fine, Lucas." She took my hand. "Don't ever change. What a stupid thing to say. You're going to change, but I wish you could stay the way you are. With that face. You still care."

"You're crying again," I said.

"I'm not! George is not worth crying over. So he's got him a new girlfriend. So he had one before me and he'll have one after her." She took another napkin and dried her eyes. "I don't care anymore. They deserve each other."

She pulled the ring off her thumb. "It's nice, isn't it? He said it was mine. Now he wants to give it to Esther."

"You don't have to give it back," I said. "He gave it to you, so it's yours."

"Yeah," she said. "You're right, Lucas." She put it back on her finger. "He can give her something else."

JERRY ASKS AN IMPORTANT QUESTION

"Hey, old son, the time is getting close," Jerry said. He was standing by the calendar counting off the days. "You're going to be going home in a week. Isn't your mother's school over on the eighteenth?"

I got up and looked at the date. I'd forgotten about the time. My uncle hadn't. He'd marked off each day.

"So is Mom ready for Michael?" he asked. "Does she know you're coming home with a dog?"

"I guess so."

"Did you ask her?"

"No, not yet."

"Don't you think you better?"

"She's going to say no. The building doesn't allow dogs."

"Hey, think positive. There are always loopholes. Believe it, or old Michael goes to the dog pound."

Was that supposed to be one of Jerry's bad jokes? Michael in a dog pound! In a cage! With people she didn't know! Not able to run. And nobody to love her. Suddenly I felt sick. Sick and stupid. And then I got scared. Where were my brains? What *was* going to happen to Michael? There were no loopholes. It wasn't Mom, it was the building. We'd lived there six years and nobody had an animal.

MOM ANSWERS THE QUESTION

I left a message for Mom to call me. Waiting for her to phone back, I kept getting these white flashes in my stomach. She was going to say yes about Michael. She was going to say no....Yes....No....Yes....

She *had* to say yes. It didn't matter about the rules. Nobody had to know about Michael. She'd sleep in my room. I'd take her out at night. I'd do everything just the way I did now.

By the time Mom called, I was so nervous I hardly gave her a chance to say hello. "I'm bringing Michael home with me," I said. "I'm coming home with her, Mom." I was almost yelling.

There was silence on her end of the line.

"You'll love her, Mom. She's trained and everything."

"Honey," Mom started. "Lucas. Sweetheart...we can't have pets, Lucas. You know the rules."

"Then we'll have to move."

"Honey, be serious."

"Mom, I am serious. Michael is my dog."

Another silence. "I'm sorry, Lucas," she said finally. "I really am, but it's impossible."

MY BRILLIANT PLAN

I grabbed Jerry's bike and rode downtown, where he was working late for a Cadillac dealer. The showroom was locked up. Everyone had gone home. But in back, a door was open, and I saw a light. Jerry was there, working on a car. He had all the doors open and the leather driver's seat out on a couple of horses. "Lucas! What's up?"

"I have this brilliant idea, Jerry. Mom says Michael can't come home with me, but look—this is home for Michael. She's happy here. So she stays with you, and I come back and see her maybe at Christmas, and then again next summer. By that time, Mom and I will have moved to a place where we can have a dog, and Michael'll come live with us."

Jerry put down a small paintbrush. "You want to leave Michael with me? What's she going to do all day when I'm working?"

"Jerry, it's not that hard. Think positive. You just change your routine a little. Run her in the morning—that's nothing for you—leave her stuff to eat, and when you come home, she can run with you again. Michael'll be company for you."

"I'm not going to do that, Lucas. I have too much going on. Anyway, I don't want a dog. I don't need a dog.

I'm sorry, Lucas. Hey, don't look that way. You know I'm sorry." He made a grab for me to give me one of his big bonding hugs.

I ducked away. "No! You can't make things better with a hug." I was having trouble breathing. "What did you give her to me for, Jerry? Why'd you do that, if you don't even like dogs?"

"You wanted her, Lucas. And she was good for you. You've had a lot of fun with her, so it worked out okay."

"And now..." I tried to hold my breath steady. I was on the edge of crying. "What do I do? What do I do now, Jerry?" I was yelling at him. I couldn't help it. "What's going to happen to Michael?"

"Lucas, I'm sorry. You want me to talk to your mother?"

"No, don't talk to Mom! She can't help it."

"I'm sorry."

"And don't say you're sorry to me ever again." I ran around the car and slammed all the doors.

Then I went home. I put Jerry's bike away in the garage. I fed Michael and took her outside. "You're the only good thing in the whole world, Michael."

Hearing her name, her ears stiffened and she came over to me. I got down and put my arms around her. She licked my face. She'd grown over the summer. She was big and warm. Every time she looked at me I felt like a murderer.

GEORGE LOSES IT

Michael and I went looking for Glori. We went to the park first and then to her house. Maybe she could keep

Michael for me. Sure she could. She had three dogs, one more wouldn't matter.

George's red pickup was parked in front of Glori's house. I walked by. I didn't want to see George. But then Boy came out, and he and Michael ran around the side of the house, and I followed.

Glori and George were in back. She was sitting on the exposed roots of an old willow tree. George was standing over her. When he saw me he threw up his arms and said, "Oh, no! What's he doing here?"

I ignored him. "Hi, Glori."

"Hi, Lucas. What do you think of this, Lucas? George wants his ring back."

"Come on, Glori," George said. "Stop wasting time. Hand it over."

"I say it's mine. A gift is a gift. What do you say, Lucas?"

"What do you care what he says?" George said.

"It's your ring to keep," I said to Glori.

She nodded. "Do you hear that, George? That's what anybody would say."

"Who's he? Who made him an expert?" He grabbed her arm, pulled her up, and tried to get the ring off her finger. She yelled and yanked free. He went after her again, and she tripped over the roots and went down.

Without thinking I put myself in front of her and stood there like a school crossing guard between her and big beefy yunko George. It was kind of stupid, but it felt great.

Then George laughed and ruined the whole thing. "Get out of here, you bug," he said, and he pushed me aside.

Michael snarled at George, defending me. I came back, and George pushed me again.

"Oh, you are such a jerk, George!" Glori said. "If you want it that bad—" She took the ring off her finger.

George stood there with a satisfied smirk on his face.

"Here," she said, "take your Cracker Jack ring."

I was hoping she'd spit on it, maybe drop it in the dirt and make him pick it up, but instead she threw it at him. Not directly, not in his face, but up in the air.

The ring sparkled. The snake eyes flashed red in the light. George was ready, hand out, palm up like an outfielder poised for an easy catch.

And then Michael leaped, her chin up, her mouth open, like a trained circus dog, and snatched the ring out of the air and caught it.

GEORGE LEARNS THE RULES

Snap! The sound of Michael's jaws closing lingered in the air. *Snap!* An instant photo: George, with his hand out, waiting. Glori, mouth open wide with delight. Michael, hovering in the air. Wonder Dog of the world.

"That dog ate my ring," George said, breaking the silence. "He swallowed it."

"She," I said.

He looked at me. "What?"

"Wonder Dog is a she," I said.

"You meatball!" George made a grab for Michael, but she was too fast for him. He went after her, but he couldn't catch her.

"What's her name?" He suddenly went soft. He got down on his hands and knees. "Here, pup," he called in his new soft voice. He held out his arms. He smiled at Michael. "Here, boy, I mean girl, good girl. Come here, baby."

Michael crouched low, hind quarters up. She growled. *Try and get me*, she seemed to say.

George sprang at her like a big brown toad grabbing for a bug. Michael leaped aside, but she was too close to the fence and George had her. "Spit it out," he ordered. He pressed her down to the ground and tried to pry her jaws open.

"Leave my dog alone." I jumped on his back.

He tried to knock me off and Michael got away.

George was so mad, he kicked the tree. Glori couldn't stop laughing. Then George took a knife out of his pocket, snapped it open, and ran after Michael. "George, are you crazy?" Glori cried.

"Run, Michael," I ordered. "Go home, girl!" That was one of the commands we'd worked on in Glori's class. Michael ran, and I ran after her.

GEORGE LEARNS
AN IMPORTANT LIFE LESSON

When George drove up to our house later, Michael was safe inside the garage with the doors locked. I was on the front steps, tossing the cigarette lighter.

"Where's the dog?" George said, jumping out of the pickup truck.

I shrugged.

"You know where he is!"

"She." I was trying to be cool, but I kept looking for Jerry to come home.

"Hey, I'm talking to you."

I tossed the lighter. I was watching his hands. Where was the knife? If he tried something, I was going to run for it.

"You scratched me," he said, pointing to his arm.

"I never touched you."

"You or your dog. If I get an infection, you're going to pay. Where's my ring?"

"You know where it is."

"Yeah. So where's the dog?"

I didn't say anything. I wasn't going to tell him, but just then Michael barked.

George tried to pull the garage door up, but I had locked it from inside. Then he really got mad, so mad his eyes turned black. He ran at me, and he was on me before I could get away. He got my foot and dragged me off the steps and halfway down to the street, just as Jerry pulled into the driveway.

"Hey!" Jerry came charging out of his car and grabbed George around the neck. "Let go," he yelled. "Let go of the boy!"

"You let go of me first," George said, but he quieted down fast. He was as big as Jerry, but he was lard to Jerry's muscle.

Then it was a three-ring circus—George demanding his ring, me trying to tell Jerry what had happened, and Jerry telling George to get away from me and stay cool.

"Give me back my ring!"

"Okay, George," Jerry said. "You're going to get your ring back. This is a problem we can solve, George. Just be patient."

"I don't feel like being patient! It's my ring and your dog ate it, and I want it now."

"I know how you feel, George." Jerry was suddenly George's best friend. "You'll get your ring, but these things take time. Sometimes in life we have to wait. My girlfriend, Kiki, says it's good to wait for things. And in a situation like this, where there's nothing to worry about—"

"Yeah," I said, "wait. Because everything is going to come out in the end." I started to laugh.

Then Jerry laughed. "I'm sorry, George, I know you don't think it's funny. But sometimes in life it's good to take a deep breath and see the humor in a situation."

MICHAEL COMES THROUGH

Michael stayed in the garage the next few days. She did her business on paper. I kept the stools lined up and in order on a piece of cardboard. The last one had the ring sticking out of it.

I called Glori, and she called George. She was there when George arrived. We were all there, including Kiki.

Jerry offered George the water hose, but he just poked the ring out with a stick and dropped it in a plastic bag.

"Are you going to tell Esther where you got the ring from?" Glori said.

George didn't answer. He didn't speak to any of us. He just got in the truck and drove away.

"I was hurting before," Glori said to Kiki, "but I feel good now. Seeing him pick up that ring was worth everything."

Kiki and Jerry went off running, and I let Michael out of the garage. She ran from Glori to me. She was so happy to be out, she was running in circles.

"Well, this was great," Glori said. "The only thing I regret now is that I didn't have my camera with me when George recovered his ring."

"I did," I said, and held up my camera.

"Lucas! Did you get his picture?"

I nodded.

"You doll!" Glori kissed Michael. "Isn't he a doll, Michael? And this dog," she said to me. "She's so smart. I'm going to really miss her."

It was the perfect time for me to ask if she'd keep Michael for me until I came back. She kept nodding as I explained everything. She was listening really carefully. I thought it meant yes.

And then she said no.

"I would, Lucas, but I'm going back to college. I can't ask my mother to take care of another dog."

"Okay," I said. What else could I say?

"What are we going to do, Lucas? We have to do something about Michael. Jerry definitely won't take her?"

I shook my head.

"That's crazy. He has to."

"He won't."

"Michael can't go to the pound." She got really upset. "There's got to be some way."

"There isn't," I said. I thought of the way I used to wish for my father, thinking if I wished hard enough he'd come home. But he never did.

"Let me think of the people I know," Glori said. She started ticking them off on her fingers.

For a moment I thought, *Yes! She's going to figure it out.*

She shook her head. "It's not going to work. I can't think of anyone. I'm just going to cry," she said. "I better leave." She rushed off, her head down. Then she came back. "I almost forgot. Lucas, I brought you a good-bye present." She reached into her bag and gave me a photo of herself and Belle.

"Thanks," I said. I wanted to say something else. I wanted to tell her that meeting her had been the best thing that had ever happened in my life. Instead, I studied the photo. I said I'd frame it when I got home and keep it on my bureau.

"I could send you a snapshot of myself. If you want it?"

"Of course I want it," she said. "Aren't you my special friend?"

I put the picture of her and Belle in my jeans pocket. Then I took it out. I didn't want her to think I'd sit on it. I put it in my shirt pocket and kept my hand over it.

JERRY COMES THROUGH, TOO

The morning I left, Kiki called up to say good-bye. "Lucas, Jerry and I are going to try to find a good home for Michael. I don't want you to worry."

Leaving Michael was the hardest thing I ever had to do in my whole life. I sat with her on the steps, talking to her. Jerry came out, and I said good-bye and put her in the garage. I didn't want her to come to the airport with me.

On the way there, Jerry didn't say much. Nothing about Michael. Maybe he thought I was still mad at him. I wasn't. It wasn't his fault. He didn't know that I was going to feel like this.

"You can drop me by the ticket counter," I said when we got to the terminal. I put out my hand. "I had a great summer, Jerry. Thanks for everything."

"Wait a minute, not so fast. You're not getting rid of me yet." He parked the car and came in all the way with me, through the security check, down the corridors to the gate, where they were already boarding my plane.

He held my hand, then gave me a hug. "It was an incredible summer, Lucas. I want you to come back. Are you coming back?"

"I guess so."

"You're coming back. You have to come back." He held my arm. "You know why? Because Michael will be here when you do."

"Excuse me?" I said.

"I'm going to keep her, Lucas. Kiki and I have been

talking. She'll run Michael in the morning, and I'll run her at night. And when I'm working, Michael can guard the house."

I kept watching his face for the joke. Why had he waited all this time to tell me? Was it true?

"So how does that strike you?" he asked. "Is that brilliant or is it brilliant?"

"Brilliant," I said. "Do you mean it?"

"I do."

"You mean it? You really mean it?"

"I do!"

"Why didn't you tell me before this? It was like torture." I was crying. "You're so stupid sometimes."

"Hey, hey, come on, guy. Awww." He started patting my back. "I'm sorry, guy. I would have told you, but I didn't know. Not until this moment. Kiki's been after me, but you know, I was kind of resisting."

I butted him. I didn't know what to say. So I did it again. I kept butting him. Then the final call came, and I threw my arms around his neck, and he landed a kiss on my head. I looked back one last time after they took the ticket. Jerry was still there, watching me. For a moment— it was like a hallucination—I thought it was my father standing there, waving like a maniac.

THE DOG IN THE FREEZER

Hey, Pop, how are you doing? I mean, where are you? I haven't heard from you since before you went down south to play winter ball. Are you back now? Are you in Arizona? I tried to call you at training camp, but they said you hadn't reported in yet.

Mom said you'd be calling me any day now. She said if I had anything to say to you, I should write it down and then put it in an envelope and mail it to you. But where am I going to send it? I've been watching the papers, but they don't say anything about Dave Estabrook, or any Cougar games either.

The newspapers should be reporting the minor leagues better. Are you playing, Pop? Are you in the regular rotation? How's the arm? Are you eating right? What about the Royals? Are they going to call you up?

You don't have to answer all these questions, Pop. Just remember, junk food affects your performance. Stay away from those tortilla corn chips.

Lots of love from your son,
Jake Estabrook

• ONE •

The Route

Jake hated to tell guys he played the violin. "You play the *violin*?" Howie Silva said, like Jake had just dipped his hands in the toilet bowl.

"I like all kinds of music," Jake said. Why did he have to say anything? He didn't have to defend the fact that he loved music. And something else he hated to talk about, to Howie or anyone else, was that his father didn't live with them anymore. His parents were breaking up—at least that's what his mother said. He didn't believe it. His father was a professional ballplayer. Baseball was his father's life, so he was away a lot because ballplayers had to go where their teams sent them.

His father hadn't been home since last Thanksgiving. He called, but it had been so long since he'd seen his father that lately Jake had been having weird thoughts. That voice on the phone: It sounded like his father—but was it really his father? It could be a recording, or a clever computer program that made all the right sounds. His father could be a prisoner in some South American country where he went to play ball every winter, and Jake wouldn't know it.

He would lie on his bed with these thoughts, his face in the pillow and his fists jammed in his stomach. It gave him a bellyache thinking about it. If it was really just his mother and him, were they even a family anymore?

His friend Howie Silva lived six blocks away and went to a private school. He also had a paper route in Jake's building that Jake was interested in. Howie said that when his family moved to Staten Island, Jake could have the route. Mornings when Howie was late delivering the papers he'd bang on Jake's door and hand him a bunch of papers. "You get the bottom ten floors. I'll get the top."

Jake liked being up early in the morning. It made him feel close to his father. When his father lived home he would get up early and run before the traffic and the fumes got so heavy you could die just from breathing.

Howie's family moved over spring vacation. Jake expected his friend to just hand him the route book. He knew the route cold. But Howie had to make a speech. He said he was offering Jake something valuable that he had built up from zilch through his own hard work and effort and blah, blah, blah. Bottom line: He wasn't giving it away for nothing. He wanted money for his route.

Jake was taken aback. Howie knew he didn't have money. That's why he wanted the route, so he could have money of his own. Besides, they were friends. Had he ever asked Howie for money all the times he'd helped him? Not once. If the route had been his and he was moving, he would have given it to Howie in a second.

"Hand over the book," he said. He was ready to grab the route book out of Howie's hands. "As soon as the customers pay me, I'll pay you." Howie would have to be satisfied with that.

• TWO •

Raoul

It was dark when Jake went out to pick up the papers. He had an old shopping cart Howie had left him. The streets were empty and quiet. Cars moved by silently. The cart creaked. Jake felt the reassuring bulk of the route book in his back pocket. It was still dark in Arizona, but he made believe his father was up now, too, and coming along with him to pick up the papers.

A skinny man stood by a white panel truck on the corner of Twenty-third Street and Lexington, just where Howie had said he'd be. It was the first time Jake was picking up the papers. He didn't know the man. "I'm here to get the papers," Jake said.

"Who are you?" The man was no taller than Jake. He wore a sweat suit with red piping and sneakers with a red stripe.

"I'm taking over Howie Silva's route."

"Says who?"

"I bought it from him."

"Whaddaya mean you bought it from him?" The man's hair was pasted down flat, and there were dark circles around his eyes. "I'm in charge." The man thumped himself on the chest. "Raoul makes the decisions. Nobody else! Raoul's the boss."

"Howie said I could have the route if I paid him."

"You're dumber than he is. You don't pay somebody for a route. If you pay, you pay me. How much did you pay?"

"Not much." The lie caught in his throat. Did the man know he hadn't paid Howie anything yet? "It doesn't matter."

"Doesn't matter?" Raoul said. "Money doesn't matter? Is that what you said? What are you here for then?"

"I didn't mean it that way."

"Give me the book," Raoul said.

Jake's heart sank as he handed it over. There went his paper route.

Raoul opened the book, turned a page, thumbed through it. "How many papers do you take?" he said. "How many dailies?" It was like a quiz. "How many Sundays? How many papers on the seventh floor? How many on the fourth?"

Jake answered all the questions correctly.

"What's your name?"

"Jacob."

"Jacob?"

"It's from the Bible."

Raoul gnawed at his fingernail. "You don't have to tell me. That's an old-time name."

"My parents picked it out," Jake said.

"No doubt," Raoul said.

• THREE •

Red-Hot Salsa

Jake waited in the lobby downstairs for his mother to come home from work. He kept going outside and looking. Fridays, she always worked late. Finally, there she was coming around the corner, hurrying, her knapsack hooked over one shoulder. "Sorry," she said, giving him a hug. "Are you starved?"

"Not exactly." He linked arms with her and they crossed the street to the market.

"Let's not spend a lot of time," she said, taking a shopping cart. "I'll get the veggies. You get the tomato sauce, and get us something for dessert."

He went speeding off.

"If it's ice cream, one pint's enough," she called after him. "Do you hear me, Jake? And no candy bars in the ice cream."

When he returned, his mother was talking to a man in a faded leather jacket. The baseball cap on his head made Jake's heart leap. For a moment, he thought it was his father. Then the man turned, and it was just a man his mother was talking to.

"This is fennel," she was explaining. She held up a fat green vegetable. "You can eat it raw."

Jake didn't like his mother talking to other men. He took her hand. "Let's go, Mom."

She glanced at the cart. "You forgot dessert, Jake."

"There's your chance, Jake," the man said, giving him a wink.

Jake had an impulse to run the cart over the man's feet. "I don't want dessert. Let's go, Mom."

At the checkout line, his mother sorted through the purchases. "What's this?" she said, holding up a jar. "Red-Hot Salsa? Who's that for?"

"Me," he said.

"It's too hot for you. Put it back."

"It's Pop's favorite."

"Maybe it is, but he's not here, is he?"

"For when he comes home." He kneed the cart forward.

"Jake," his mother said. "You have to get real. Your father will come to see you, but we're not living together anymore. Things have changed."

Jake heard her, but as far as he could see, things were just about the way they'd always been. His father went away and his mother got mad, but then he came back, and things went back to the way they'd been. When his father came home, his parents would talk and then they got happy, and they all went to the ocean together. His mother liked to collect shells, and he and his father liked to smash into the big waves.

Jake stacked their purchases by the cash register. He put the jar of Red-Hot Salsa in front so his mother could see it. She didn't say anything. That proved he was right. His father was coming home.

In the house, his mother made supper while he practiced the violin. When the spaghetti was ready, Jake put the violin down in its velvet case on the chair next to him, where he could look at it. There were times when music made him so happy he couldn't hold still. It made him want to dance and do somersaults and run down the middle of Third Avenue.

"Jake." His mother brought the pot to the table and sat down. "Are you still upset? You know, I've talked about this. Your father and I haven't been getting along for a long time. Remember when we followed him, Jake? Remember the buses and living in motels? You always got sick on those buses. It was no life."

"Once he goes to the Royals, we can live in Kansas City."

"Jake, you're dreaming. It's not going to happen, honey."

"You just don't want to live in Kansas City. Maybe he'll go to the Yankees, and we'll stay right here. You'll like that. Once he makes it to the majors—"

"Jake! Jake, cut it out."

He wiped his hands and picked his violin up. He blew on the wood, then polished it with the napkin. Playing in the majors was like playing in an orchestra with all the best players in the world. That's where his father belonged. The majors. Everyone would know him then. His name and his picture would be in the paper and on TV all the time. And then he would live in one place, and his mother would change her mind, and he and she would go live with his father.

Hey, Pop, remember last Thanksgiving when you were home? Just before you left for the winter leagues? Remember how you and Mom couldn't agree? Remember how you wanted turkey and Mom said she wasn't going to eat anything live? Or cook it? Remember the Chinese restaurant? It was like a red dragon inside, down in the basement of that old building. You didn't want to go in, but it was good. We had turkey chow mein and Mom had tofu and vegetables.

Remember the fortune cookies? Mine said, MONEY IS VERY IMPORTANT TO YOU. And I said, "Yeah, I love money." And you and Mom laughed. Well, speaking of money, I got a job. I've got a newspaper route. It's all in our building. I put the papers in the elevator and take them to the twentieth floor. Then I work my way down, floor by floor. I don't even have to go out, except to get the papers.

You should hear the boss. He said if I forgot to do my route even once, I was out. He said if I got sick and I didn't tell him, I was out. He said if a customer complained about me, I was out.

I said, "Three strikes and you're out," but he didn't get the joke, Pop. He's not a baseball man.

Pop, remember what your fortune cookie said? EXPECT IMPORTANT DECISIONS IN YOUR LIFE. You know what that means? This is your year, Pop. You're going to have to make a MAJOR decision. Get it, Pop? Kansas City. Maybe Chicago. Maybe the Yankees! Fortune cookies never lie, Pop.

Lots of love from your son,
Jake Estabrook

• FOUR •

Paperboy

Fridays, Jake left his customers a little brown envelope with the newspaper. Then, Saturdays, he rang the bell. "Paperboy, collecting," he said. It was a simple technique. All the customer had to do was open the door and hand him the envelope with the money in it.

Some people did. Sometimes they had a cookie for him, and kept him there talking. Mrs. Alyce always overpaid him and said keep the change. She was one of the nice people. The not-so-nice ones barely opened the door.

"Paperboy, collecting."

"Who?" The door opened a crack. The chain was in

place. A squinty, suspicious eye peered out. "Who are you? You're not the regular boy."

"I'm the new paperboy," Jake said. "Jake Estabrook."

"What?" Like "paperboy" was a new word in the English language. Like it wasn't even English.

"Collecting," he said. He had to pay Raoul for the papers every week, and if he didn't collect, the money for next week's paper was coming out of his pocket. "Collecting," he said again. He had his receipt pad ready.

The not-so-nice ones said come back next week because they didn't have the money or the right change, even though they knew Jake came that same time every week.

5G was the worst. Mr. Kleiner lived there. He was a very big man. For a while, Jake thought he was a retired wrestler. Oscar, the doorman, told Jake that Mr. Kleiner was a retired accountant. He had white hair down over his collar and black, bristly eyebrows with stray white hairs poking out.

His dog looked just like him. The same bristly eyebrows and the same mean expression. Only in miniature. The dog was the size of a burp, but he had the bark of a lion. Jake was glad the door was between them. Every morning when Jake dropped the paper, the dog snarled as if he were going to burst through the door.

Then Jake would hear Mr. Kleiner. "Shut up, barfbag! You piece of garbage, get over here."

"Collecting." Tuesday night, Jake stood in front of 5G. He'd missed Mr. Kleiner on Saturday. He could hear the dog sniffing on the other side of the door even before he rang the bell.

Mr. Kleiner opened the door, and the dog shot out from behind his legs like a bullet. He was all teeth and growl. Jake jumped back. He didn't want to, but he couldn't help himself. "Collecting, sir!"

The dog bristled and bounced, like a hairbrush with feet.

"Nice doggy, nice doggy!"

He lunged at Jake's ankles. The hairs on his gray muzzle stood straight out.

Jake danced to save his life. Mr. Kleiner watched as if Jake were putting on a show.

The dog's teeth were shiny, white, and wet, and he was spitting foam. Mr. Kleiner finally picked him up by the scruff. "What's the matter with you, you dried-up little fart." He threw the dog inside and shut the door.

They were both inside, and Jake was outside. He hadn't gotten paid again—it was two weeks now—but he didn't care. He was glad to get away alive.

FIVE

Nelson

If 5G was the worst, 7A was the best. That was where the Martinezes lived with their dog, Nelson. Connie Martinez was one of Jake's best friends, and his very best friend in the building. Her father was a painting contractor and kept his ladders and paint tarps in the basement. He let Jake keep his newspaper cart there, too.

When Jake collected, Nelson always came to the door with Connie. Nelson was a big, creased, friendly beagle. He loved company. While Connie went for the money, Jake squatted down and talked to him. "Nelson, are you going to bite me?" He put his hand in Nelson's mouth. "Friends don't eat each other."

"I can't talk to you now," Connie said, coming back with the money. She had bangs and wore glasses that magnified her dark eyes. "The book I'm reading is too exciting."

Jake saw Connie again the next afternoon, on his way home through Madison Park. He'd bought a plant in the flower district and it was sticking out of his knapsack. Nelson was in the dog run chasing around with some other dogs. "Nice plant," Connie said.

"It's for my mother's birthday." Jake stood there, watching Nelson. "He's having a good time," he said. They talked about Nelson, and he told her about Mr. Kleiner's dog.

Connie didn't think she knew him. "What's his name? I know all the dogs in our building."

"I don't think he has a name."

"What does 5G call him?"

"You don't want to hear."

"Is he small and dark and totally crazy and nervous?" Close up, Connie's eyes could be hypnotic. "Small dogs always bark a lot," she said. Her eyes left no room for disagreement. "That's the way they get respect."

"Who's going to respect that cockroach?"

"There's something lovable about every dog." She pushed back the sleeves of her sweatshirt. It was oversized and came down to her knees.

"You think all dogs are nice because of Nelson."

When Nelson heard his name mentioned, he came over and sat at Jake's feet. Jake scratched his head.

"Don't let him near your mother's plant," Connie said. "He chews up everything."

"You're not going to chew up my plant, are you, Nelson?" Jake said. "Nelson's an old pussycat." Jake pulled him around like a big stuffed pillow. "This is an easy dog to like."

"Did you ever try giving that little dog in 5G a smile?" Connie said.

"Did you ever smile through a door?"

"Well, you could say something nice to him. If you want Mr. Kleiner's dog to like you—"

"Who said I did?" He rubbed Nelson's head hard. "That dog hates me."

Connie gave him the big look. "Are you afraid of him, Jake?"

"No way," he said, but he avoided her eyes. He wasn't going to admit that he was scared of a dog he could put in his pocket.

SIX

Big Boy

The next few mornings when Jake dropped Mr. Kleiner's paper, the dog had his usual fit, snarling and clawing at the door. But instead of rushing past, Jake lingered. "Hi," he said through the door. "Remember me?"

The dog hit the door like a battering ram.

"This is Jake Estabrook. How're you doing today?"

The dog barked like a machine gun. It sounded like he was going to blow himself up.

Jake waited until he stopped. "Wow," he said, "that was great. You're some barker."

One day, returning from school, Jake saw Mr. Kleiner's dog in the elevator. He hesitated to get on, even though

Mr. Kleiner had the dog on a leash. "In or out?" Mr. Kleiner said.

Reluctantly, Jake got on.

"What floor?" Mr. Kleiner said.

"Fifteen, please. Thank you." Mr. Kleiner pushed the button. He didn't want Mr. Kleiner to think he didn't like him and his dog.

On the way up, the dog was perfect. He didn't bark. He kept back behind Mr. Kleiner. No snarls or anything. In fact, he looked half cute tucked in behind Mr. Kleiner's big feet. Even a little shy, maybe.

"Hey, little dog," Jake said softly.

The dog looked up at him and smiled. Not a big smile, just white teeth arranged in a pleasant half-moon. The elevator stopped on the fifth floor, and Mr. Kleiner got off with the dog. "See you," Jake called after them.

On Thursday, when Jake delivered the paper, the dog scratched and sniffed under the crack of the door. He didn't bark. "Good little dog," Jake said. He was going to have to tell Connie her method really worked. "Good little dog," he said again. Maybe he shouldn't call him little. Nobody liked to be called little. He still remembered how, when he was little, he always wanted to be bigger and see what was on the table or do what the big people were doing.

"How're you doing, Big Boy?"

The dog stopped scratching at the door. He was listening.

"Big Boy," Jake said, even though the dog was no bigger than a dried-out prune. "You like that name, don't you, Big Boy? Hey, big dog," he said softly, "it's Jake Estabrook."

The dog was clawing the door again.

"You're going to wear your nails off scratching like that, Big Boy." He thought the dog was responding to his voice and he kept it calm and even.

After that, every time Jake said Big Boy, the dog stopped and listened. It was a good sign. It meant they were getting to be friends.

SEVEN

The Phone Call

Jake was on his way out of the apartment when the phone rang. He turned back and picked it up.

"Is this the world-famous Jake Estabrook?"

"Pop!" Jake dropped his knapsack. His face flamed. "Where are you?" His father's voice sounded as if he were right here in the building, downstairs in the lobby, using the house phone and winking at the doorman. "Are you here?"

"I'm out here in God's country: Sand Creek, Arizona," his father said in his slow, unhurried voice. "Right now, Jake, I'm in a telephone booth on the side of the road. Nobody here but me and the jackrabbits. I sure wish you were here with me. I just finished running, and I thought, What time is it back there? What's my son doing right now? I want to hear his voice."

Jake glanced at the clock. He'd be late for school, but he didn't care. This was more important than school, more important than anything.

"So how are you doing?" his father said. "I haven't talked to you in a while. How's school? How's it moving?"

"Okay." He had all this stuff he'd been thinking about to say to his father, but now he couldn't think of a single thing. "What about the team, Pop?"

"The last game against Sanora, not so good. My concentration was way off. The game before, against Billings, I was terrific. Estabrook, the man of the hour! They got three hits off me in five innings. Fifty-five pitches, and that's all those suckers got."

Jake couldn't shake the thought that in a minute his father would walk into the apartment, throw down his bag, and say, *Let's go, Jake, let's go to the ocean.*

"You're pitching good, Pop. You're getting better all the time."

"I've been cut," his father said.

"Cut, Pop?" He knew what it meant.

"Cut from the roster," his father said. "Cut from the team."

"Are you teasing me, Pop?"

"The manager said I could go down to Fort Defiance. I said no, thanks, I'm not going down. No more. I'm too old for that stuff. I told him, I go up or I'm out. So I'm out."

"Pop, they can't cut you."

"There's no such thing as can't. They can cut anybody they want to. They think I'm too old, but I'm not that old. Don't worry, I'm working on some things. Confidence, that's the key. I'm not done yet."

How could they cut his father? His father was too good, too valuable. His father was a great pitcher. He had been on the Eagles and the Hawks and the Royals had had him up for six days.

"You're going to come back, Pop."

"Yeah," his father said. A heavy silence settled over the line. "Is your mother there? How's she doing?"

"She's at work."

"You don't have to say anything about this to her yet."

"Okay, Pop."

"What I can't figure out," his father said, after a moment, "I was pitching good. I had a couple of bad games. You can't be on top of your game all the time."

"That's the truth, Pop. Every pitcher has good days and bad days."

When his father spoke again, he seemed to have forgotten Jake. "I've given my life to the game. You give your life to the game, you think you belong to it, and then in a flash you're out. I don't get it."

"You're going to get another team, Pop. The Royals. Don't forget the Royals. They need you."

"Jake, you're the greatest kid in the world," his father

said. "You're the best thing in my life. I love you, son."

"I love you, too, Pop," Jake said. He wanted to jump into the phone and swim or fly or do whatever you do when you're in a telephone line to come out where his father was.

It was only after he hung up that he realized he hadn't asked his father for his address. He didn't even know where to call him.

• EIGHT •

The Bite

Saturday morning, when Jake went to collect, Mr. Kleiner opened the door and let the dog out. At first Big Boy just snuffled around Jake's feet. Jake acted natural, but it wasn't easy. He felt needles going up and down the back of his legs.

"What do I owe you?" Mr. Kleiner said.

"Three weeks. Remember, Mr. Kleiner, you didn't pay me last week and the week before?"

"Okay, yeah, I know." He went inside, shut the door, and left the dog outside in the hall with Jake.

The dog was quiet. They were looking at each other, and then Jake made the mistake of being friendly. "How you doing, Big Boy?"

The dog flattened himself against the floor and growled deep in his throat.

Jake didn't move. He didn't want to excite the dog. He wished Mr. Kleiner would hurry up. "Mr. Kleiner!" he called.

That was like a signal. Big Boy leaped. Jake thought he was going straight for his throat, and he put his arm out. It was a reflex, but it came out like a karate chop. The dog went flying back. Then he came at Jake again and got his teeth into Jake's jeans, and hung on there, growling deep in his throat. He was like a snapping turtle, the kind that never lets go, even if you cut its head off.

Jake shook his leg, tried to knock the dog loose. He didn't remember screaming, but maybe he did, because all of a sudden people were popping out of their apartments up and down the hall.

Mr. Kleiner charged out and grabbed the dog. He shoved money into Jake's hand and glared at everyone else. "What are you morons looking at? You think this is a Broadway show?" He went inside and slammed the door.

"You all right, dear?" a woman in a white suit said. She looked like a nurse. "That's a terrible dog."

Jake nodded bravely and limped toward the stairs. He was wounded. He was sure blood was running down his leg.

On the stairs, he examined his leg. His pants were torn, but there was no blood. He rubbed his leg. *Die, dog!* He tried a couple of practice kicks to see if he was okay. Then he did a full kickoff, like he was getting ready to send the football through the end zone. Only the football was Big Boy. Jake imagined how he'd send the dog flying. He'd launch him, like a rocket, straight up, past the limits of the earth's gravitational pull, out the other end of the universe.

• NINE •

The Wog Is Wed

"My nose is dwippy." It was Connie, on the phone. "I widn't go to school today," she said in a croaky voice.

"You sound great," Jake said. He was tightening his violin bow.

"Mr. Kweiner's wog is wed."

"What?"

"Mr. Kweiner had him wapped up in newspapers," she sniffled.

"Newspapers?"

"In the ewevator. He was bwinging the wog down to the incinewator room."

"Who?"

"The wog," she said thickly. "Mr. Kweiner's wog is wed."

"Mr. Kleiner's dog is dead?" Jake didn't believe her. "I just saw him on Saturday. He bit me. My leg still hurts."

"He bid you?"

"Not much. Just a little. He's not dead."

"You don't bewieve me?"

"No."

"Thanks. You're pwobabwy wight. The wog is upstairs, sitting at the table with Mr. Kweiner wight now, weading the newspaper." Connie started laughing, then choked, then couldn't speak at all.

"Anyway, it's not my dog," Jake said, and he hung up.

Standing at the window, he let the bow move over the strings of the violin. He played a little tune that moved like the uneven ups and downs of buildings and roofs. In the distance, an American flag hung at half-mast, barely stirring in the wind. Somebody important must have died. Big Boy!

He played a major scale. Then a minor one. Big Boy, dead? Was he really dead? He could still hear the dog snarling and feel his teeth in his leg.

Maybe Connie just thought he was dead because Mr. Kleiner had him wrapped in newspapers. Mr. Kleiner could have been bringing him to the vet. Things weren't always what they seemed. People might say Jake's father didn't care about him, because they never saw them together, but they'd be wrong.

Jake practiced his scales, one after another. Then he

took a break and called Mr. Kleiner's number. There were some things you had to find out for yourself. The phone rang a couple of times.

"Hello!"

"Uh, hello. Mr. Kleiner, uh—"

"Who is this?"

"Is your dog okay?"

"What business is it of yours?"

Jake was sorry he hadn't disguised his voice. "I heard your dog died. He didn't die, did he?"

"Maybe you want to pay for a funeral? I can arrange that."

Jake hung up fast.

A little later, there was a knock at the door, and he almost dove into the closet, he was so sure it was Mr. Kleiner.

"Jake, open up!" It was Connie.

Jake opened the door. "The dog's dead," he said.

"I towd you." She held her hand to her nose. It looked red and sore. "Give me a dissue."

Jake handed her a paper towel. "I called Mr. Kleiner."

"Did he say he was wed?"

"No. But he is. I could tell. Weird."

"I'm sowwy he's wed. I feel bad. I hade it when a wog wies."

Jake nodded. He felt bad, too. He didn't know why.

TEN

The Incinerator Room

The incinerator room was in the second basement. It was hot and airless. The corridor was in shadows. The elevator motors whined. Big Boy was lying under newspapers on the floor, legs stuck out. His head was covered.

Jake lifted the edge of the paper. The dog didn't look dead. He seemed to be asleep. His hair was black and bristly and his ears were as sharp as ever. Jake squatted and touched the dog with the tip of his finger. The hair on his side was rough, but the belly hair was soft. He touched the dog again, and he stirred, he definitely moved. He was warm. He seemed to quiver and sigh.

Jake stayed there, waiting. Would Big Boy move again?

He lay there, motionless. "I didn't want you to die," Jake said. "I didn't hate you. I never hated you, just when you bit me."

It was true. He'd said *die*, but he hadn't meant it. It was just something he said because the dog came at him so fast and scared him and made him want to strike back. There had been times he had said things to his mother that he didn't really mean. Once he'd even wished his father's sore pitching arm wouldn't heal, so he'd have to stay home longer. They were just things he thought sometimes. He never meant them to really happen.

He kept hoping the dog would wake up. Was Big Boy holding his breath—faking it? He remembered his father's trick of lying on the floor and playing dead. That was when Jake was little. He'd shake his father, pull his hair, but he never moved. Then, just as Jake began to cry, his father would jump up, bear-hug him, and call him a soft-hearted sucker.

The incinerator room was full of cans and soda bottles in black plastic bags for recycling, and stacks of papers and magazines. The super had told Jake that Sanitation sent a special truck when an animal died, but that they all ended up in the same place in the same landfill, with all the rest of the garbage.

A dog wasn't garbage, though. It wasn't something you used and then threw away. The dog was part of Mr. Kleiner's family. He'd been a good guard dog. He probably loved Mr. Kleiner. Maybe. Mr. Kleiner didn't act very loving, but maybe he loved Big Boy anyway. Loved him

111

in a rough way. Jake's father was like that a little bit. He liked to play rough, but he really loved him. Not the way his mother did, of course. There were just different ways people loved.

"Well, I'll go now, Big Boy." He lingered, though, still hoping the dog would move. He wouldn't even care if it jumped up and showed its teeth. But it didn't do anything. Finally he said, "Good-bye, Big Boy," and left.

At the elevator, he heard something and ran back one last time. The dog was lying there. Sometimes people went into a coma and didn't wake up for days, weeks even. And then one day they woke up and looked around and said, *How are you all doing today?*

What if the dog woke in the middle of the night and didn't know where he was? What if it didn't wake up till the special truck came? What if he woke inside the compactor, and the motor was going and they couldn't hear him barking?

Jake picked up the dog. He didn't know he was going to do it till he did it. He wrapped the dog in newspapers. He was surprised how light it was. It didn't weigh anything.

In the lobby, two people got on the elevator. Jake kept the dog hidden in his arms. Upstairs, he got lucky. His mother was in the shower, and he brought the dog into his room and shut the door.

ELEVEN

The Heating Pad

Jake folded a blanket under the dog. He moved its legs and blew in its face. He pressed the dog's soft belly. "Breathe," Jake said softly. He was doing the CPR the way his mother had practiced on him when she took the Red Cross class for her job. When he pressed, the dog breathed, but when he stopped, the breathing stopped.

Jake knocked on the bathroom door. "Mom? Where's the heating pad?"

She opened the door. Her wet hair lay flat around her face. "What happened? Did you hurt yourself?"

"No, it's an experiment," Jake said.

"For school?"

"Uh-huh." It was half true. If the dog woke up, Jake would have a fantastic story to tell his friends in school.

He plugged in the heating pad and covered Big Boy with it so only his bristly little face showed. Then he went to the kitchen, got a piece of bread, and filled a bowl with water.

"Don't eat now," his mother called. "We're having supper soon."

Jake locked the door to his room. He tore the bread into small pieces and put them near the water dish. Then he lay on his bed and watched the dog. He imagined him waking up, sniffing the water and bread, then sousing Jake. If he got mean, Jake would just have to remind him of a few basic facts, starting with who'd saved his life.

He touched Big Boy. He was warm now. "Big Boy," he said softly. He'd always wanted to have someone to talk to, especially at night when he woke up and the room was dark and there were shapes and things in the corners.

"Breathe," he ordered. He punched the pillow hard so the dog would hear him. "Breathe!" *Whomp!* Into the pillow. Like his father's pitches into the catcher's mitt. Leather hitting leather. Ninety miles an hour. Dust kicking up. *Whomp!* Jake punched the pillow. It was going to happen. He was making it happen. The dog was going to wake up.

He held one of the dog's paws and moved it around, so it was more comfortable. Was he alive? Touching something dead was creepy. "Big Boy, can you hear me? Wake up."

"Jake...Jacob." His mother was at the door. "Who are you talking to? Open up, Jake. I haven't seen you all day."

"Okay, wait a minute." Jake carefully pushed the dog under the bed. Then he opened the door.

"Why do you have the door locked?" his mother said, coming in. She was wrapped in a blue terry-cloth robe and wore gorilla slippers. "What's the smell in here?"

Jake fanned the air. "What smell?" He opened the window.

"Oh, honey, close that! My head's wet and it's cold outside." She pulled the sheets straight on his bed and smoothed the blanket. "How about a hug?" She kissed him. "You smell like something burning. Have you been playing with matches?"

"Mom, I'm not a baby." He was worried about the smell. If she kept sniffing around, she was going to find Big Boy. "When are we going to eat?"

"What have you eaten since you came home?"

"Nothing."

"Give me five minutes. I'll make something."

When she left, he checked under the bed. Big Boy's head had slipped off his paws. Jake rearranged him again so he looked more comfortable. "If you wake up," he said, "I'll just be in the next room."

His mother was chopping peppers and tomatoes for an omelet. The smell of onions frying in a pan made him hungry. She brought the omelet to the table with hot pita bread and sliced cucumbers.

"I don't know why a chiropractor's office is such a

madhouse on Friday," she said. "Maybe people want to feel good so they can wreck themselves over the weekend." She brought him a napkin. "You aren't going to like this, but I have to work tomorrow. "

"I thought we were going to do something." Jake got the jar of salsa from the cupboard and spooned some on the omelet.

"It's just the morning." She cleaned out the sink and put the garbage in a plastic bag. "We'll have the afternoon. How can you taste anything with that junk all over it?"

He poured on more salsa. "You don't like it, but I like it, and Pop likes it, too." He hadn't said anything to his mother about his father being cut from the team. He was hoping his father would call soon with good news. Maybe he was on the phone to Kansas City right now. "I hope Pop's shoulder doesn't tighten up the way it did last year."

She didn't reply. "I'm going out tonight with Lucy," she said. "Just the two of us. Okay?"

"Okay."

"You don't mind?"

"Don't mind."

She put her face close to his. "You've got salsa on your face." She tried to wipe it off, but he pushed her hand away.

116

When he went back to his room, there was definitely a smell, but the exciting thing was that Big Boy had moved. Jake was positive. The dog had been lying with his head on his paws. Now he was on his side.

• TWELVE •

The Dog in the Freezer

"He's in my room," Jake said when Connie opened the door to her apartment.

"Who is?" She was reading a book.

"The *dog* is," he said, stepping into the narrow hallway.

"What dog? What are you talking about?" Connie said. She was speaking normally again.

"The dog. Mr. Kleiner's dog. He's under my bed. I can't stay long. I think he's going to wake up."

"You took a dead dog into your apartment? Are you crazy, Jake?"

"He's not definitely dead." Jake looked into the living room. Mr. Martinez was sitting on the couch with his hands over his eyes. "What's the matter with your father?"

"He just parked the car." Connie pushed Jake toward the door, whispering, "Put the dog back where you found it."

"I can't. They'll throw him in the garbage."

"Jake. Jake." She sounded exactly like his mother. "The dog is dead. What difference does it make where he goes?"

"I told you, he's probably going to wake up."

"Oh, sure. And then he'll bite you."

"No he won't. I saved his life. He'll be grateful."

"Then you'll have to give him back to Mr. Kleiner. It's his dog."

"Not anymore. He threw him away. Finder's keepers, he's my dog now."

They stood in the dark hall. There was a shine in her large eyes. "I admire you for what you're trying to do, Jake. But you know he's not going to wake up." She was whispering, and she shook his arm. "He's dead, Jake. Right now, in your room. Don't feel bad. Dying is natural." She was like a teacher sometimes. "If you live, you're going to die. Everything living dies. Dogs die. Cats die. Goldfish die."

Families die. It just popped into his head. He hated the thought. "I got to go," he said.

118

Upstairs, Big Boy was lying where he'd left him with his head on the newspaper. The smell was bad. Really bad. Jake opened the window, then stood looking down at the dog. His eyes were closed. They weren't just shut— they were *sealed* shut. He felt suddenly like the worst thing in the world had just happened. He wished he could call his father and talk to him.

He put the dog into a black plastic bag. Now that he knew Big Boy was dead, he didn't want to touch him anymore. But he didn't want to bring the dog back to the incinerator room, either. He didn't know what he was going to do. He went into the kitchen and emptied the freezer and put the dog all the way in the back. Then he replaced the frozen dinners and the bagels and the pint of Wavy Gravy ice cream.

• THIRTEEN •

Reincarnation

Jake was in his pajamas and watching TV when his mother and Lucy came in. They were laughing a lot, which meant that they'd had some beers. "Are you decent, Jacob?" Lucy said. She and his mother both laughed.

Lucy sat down next to him on the couch and gave him a hug. She wore baggy flowered pants and a military style shirt. Jake liked Lucy, but she was grabby. "Wouldn't I love to have a boy like you." It was the same thing she always said.

His mother put water on to heat and put out cups and the tea bags. "Want some cocoa, Jake? Do we have any graham crackers left, honey? I feel like an ice cream and graham cracker sandwich."

Jake sprang to his feet. "I'll get it, Mom." He got the ice cream from the freezer and shut the door fast.

"Ooof, what stinks in there?" Lucy said.

"I don't smell anything," Jake said.

"It could be the stove," Lucy said. "Is your pilot light out? That could cause a smell."

His mother tried all the burners. Then she got on a chair and sniffed around the exhaust vent over the stove. "It's probably coming from another apartment."

"I keep my vent taped up to keep the smells and roaches out," Lucy said.

"Does that work?"

"No, but it makes me feel better."

They laughed again. Then they sat on the floor eating ice-cream sandwiches like a couple of girls.

"Are funerals expensive?" Jake asked. "What would it cost to bury somebody small?"

"Do you mean like a child?" his mother said. "What have you been watching on TV? I don't want you to think about those things."

"Seriously, Mom, what if someone dies and nobody knows who they are? What happens? Who takes them? Who buries them?"

"Don't die in the street," Lucy said. "Big mistake, Jake. They'll stop and look, then they'll step over you and walk away. If you have to die, wait till you get home."

"Or call somebody first," his mother said.

"Oh, I know who *I'd* call," Lucy said. "'Hello, ex-husband. I'm going to be dying in a couple of minutes.

Come pick up my body. The body you cast off.'"

That started them laughing again, and they couldn't stop.

"You didn't answer the question," Jake said.

Lucy fixed her round little eyes on him. "You'll never die, Jake. Don't be afraid."

"Lucy," his mother said. "You're not talking to a six-year-old. He doesn't want to hear a lot of fairy tales. I've always told him the truth."

"Yes," Lucy said. "Part of you does die, but I'm talking about the essence, the thing that makes you *you*." She was waving her arms, shaping the big picture. "There's part of you that never dies—the spiritual part, your soul; it changes form, but it's always present."

"You mean reincarnation," Jake said.

"Wait a minute," his mother interrupted. She had a cigarette out. The only time she smoked were the nights she drank beer. "Lucy, do you really think it's possible? That I was Cleopatra in another life? What a great idea. But next time I'm coming back as a twenty-story building."

"Sorry, nothing man-made. You don't have to come back in human form, but it has to be something that lived. A tree, a bird, a butterfly, something with wings."

"But what happens if you die and nobody knows you?" Jake was disgusted with both of them. It was a simple question. "Who buries you?"

"Don't worry, sweetheart," Lucy said. "If it's you, Jacob, you'll get wings and fly straight to heaven."

• FOURTEEN •

Freezer Dog

The next morning, when Jake did his paper route, he skipped Mr. Kleiner. He didn't do it intentionally. He started to throw a paper down, and then he couldn't. It didn't seem right without the dog there.

When he went back upstairs, his mother had already left for work. He checked the freezer, but nothing had been moved. He got out the Cheerios and a bowl.

The phone rang. "Hello," a man said, "is Jan there?"

"Who?"

"Jan."

"Who's this?" Jake said.

"Have I got her name wrong? Jan, Nan, whatever. Is

she there?" The man had a deep, scratchy voice, like he smoked a lot.

Jake didn't say anything.

"Hello. Hello," the man said. "You still there?"

"Yes."

"I want to talk to Jan. Who am I talking to here?"

"Jake."

"Well, Jake, just tell her the guy with the darts called."

The phone rang again as Jake was getting the raisins. He threw them one at a time into the bowl. "Darts," he muttered to himself.

The phone continued ringing. Jake poured the milk into the bowl and got a spoon. Finally he picked up the phone.

"Where were you, in the bathroom?" Connie said.

"I'm eating." He read her the ingredients off the cereal box.

"Fascinating," Connie said. "Did your mother make you get rid of the dog?"

"She didn't say a word about it."

"She's letting you keep a dead dog in the house?"

"In the kitchen, if you want to know."

"Next thing, you'll tell me he's playing the violin."

"He's in the freezer."

"That's good, Jake. You're working on your comedy routine."

"He's in the freezer," he repeated.

"You put the dog in the freezer? Wait a minute while I throw up. I've got to see this."

She was there in a few moments, wearing a giant Mickey Mouse sweatshirt. "Let's see him." He opened the freezer door. "I don't see him."

He pulled some things aside and pointed to the black plastic bag.

"What are you showing me?" Connie said.

"That's him."

"That?" She grabbed the bag.

He came sliding out and fell with a thump on the floor. Big Boy's head stuck out. Ice clung to its muzzle. Connie backed away, her hand over her mouth.

Jake stared at the dead thing lying on the floor. At this thing that had once been Big Boy, but wasn't anymore.

Connie wiped her eyes. "I'm sorry for you, Jake. You tried so hard to be his friend. If he hadn't died, you would have succeeded. I really think so."

His eyes filled. They were tearing and he had to blow his nose. He looked around for a tissue.

"You know what?" Connie said.

"What?" He blew his nose.

"You're really crazy, Jake!" She'd been feeling so sorry for him, but now she was pointing her finger and chanting, "You froze a dead dog! You—"

"I know. Not too smart," he admitted.

"No, don't say that! I would say it was supersmart." She ran around to the other side of the table so she wouldn't have to look at the dog. "This is something new, Jake, a real discovery, something for the whole world. Freeze your dog when it dies! Freezer Dog. This is the greatest discovery since Newton got hit in the head with an apple."

When Connie got going this way, she couldn't stop herself. "Frozen Freezer Pet. Keep him next to Kool Kat. Want an instant pet? Take Freezer Dog out and thaw him. You never have to feed him or take him to the toilet. Just defrost your pet and play with him. When you're done, put him back in the freezer."

She circled the room. "You outdid yourself this time, Jake. This is not eating a banana with your mouth open. This is number one, top of the line, supervomit. What's next? What do we do now?"

Jake got the aluminum foil from behind the stove and unrolled it completely. The truth was, he couldn't stand looking at the dog either.

Connie watched him closely. "Are you going to cook it, Jake? Is that your plan? Have a special treat for your mother when she comes home. Are we all going to get a chance to taste it? Then are you going to sell the bones to a scientific supply house? You could make yourself a tidy sum."

He rolled the dog up in the aluminum foil. It wasn't a dog anymore. It was something stiff and hard, like a piece of iron. He wound the aluminum foil around it till it disappeared and looked like a shiny silver mummy.

In the hall closet he dug out one of his father's old Syracuse University sport bags, orange with black letters. He put the dog into the bag, stuffed newspapers around it to keep it from bouncing around, and zipped it shut.

"Now what, Jake?" Connie said.

He didn't know exactly. First he had to get it out of the house. Then he'd think of something. They went out into the hall and Jake locked the door.

"Where are we going to go? You can't just walk around the city with a dead dog. Are you going to throw him in a Dumpster?"

"No." He was never going to "throw" the dog anywhere, he was sure of that. "I'm going to bury him," he said, pressing the elevator button. That's what you did with dead things. You buried them.

"Oh, good. I hate it when people flush their pets away. Even a little goldfish or a mouse. Animals are human in a way, every living thing is human."

Jake nodded. Sometimes Connie said things he really liked.

"But where are you going to bury it? You can't even bury a person in the city. They go to New Jersey or Long Island. Have you been to a dog funeral in New York lately?"

"I don't go to funerals," he said. "My mom says they're not for kids."

"Mine, too," Connie said. "Mom says it's a part of growing up I can do without."

• FIFTEEN •

Pet Rest

They went upstairs so Connie could get a jacket. Mr. Martinez was sitting at the table reading the papers. "Dad, can I wear your jacket?" Connie said. She already had it on. It was a Washington Redskins jacket.

"Where you going?" he said. "Your mother went over to see your sister."

"Going for a walk."

"Maybe your father's got an idea," Jake whispered. He motioned to the bag. "But don't tell him."

"Dad, I want to ask you something." She went over and started examining her father's hair. "What are we going to do when Nelson dies?"

He looked up. "Why? Is there a reason we're talking about it now?"

"Nelson's going to die someday; we need to think about it. Are we going to bury him?"

"I suppose so."

"Well, where?"

"Where? I don't know where. I haven't thought about it. Do I have to give you an answer this minute? Where is Nelson, anyway?" He looked at Jake. "Did you kids do something to that dog? What's going on?"

"Dad, relax," Connie said. "Nelson's by the TV having a snooze. Jake and I were having a little discussion, and all I want to know is, when Nelson gets old and dies, what do we do with him?"

Connie's father sat back and laced his hands behind his head. "Connie, when the old dog dies, we'll do right by him. We'll have a funeral…a procession…maybe twenty, thirty cars. One car just for flowers, and a motorcycle police escort. We'll cross the East River and go to the Pet Rest out past Long Island City. Father Reo will pronounce 'ashes to ashes and dust to dust.' The whole family will be there. You, me, Mom, your sister. Do you want to invite Jake? Jake can come, too. Everyone will get a free embroidered handkerchief to cry into."

Jake stared at Mr. Martinez. It was just like listening to Connie, the same sense of humor.

"The grave will be covered with flowers, and in time, a nice stone will be bought and put into place. The kind of stone a dog would appreciate. It will be shaped like a dog bone and it will be six feet tall. It will say 'Nelson, Beloved Dog, Beloved Friend, Beloved Pet, Rest in Peace Always.'"

"Dad, you're hopeless." Connie bumped Jake toward the door. "Let's go."

• SIXTEEN •

A Football Pass

Going down, the elevator stopped at the fifth floor and Mr. Kleiner got on. Connie gave Jake a look. He pushed the bag back behind him, but it was too late: Mr. Kleiner had seen it. He was looking right at the bag. He pointed, pinning Jake to the spot. "That bag!" he said, fixing Jake with his deep, penetrating X-ray eyes. Jake was sure he saw the dog through all its wrappings.

"The bag!" Mr. Kleiner repeated.

Jake stood rigid as a pole. Next, Mr. Kleiner was going to say, *Open that bag!* He'd make Jake take the dog out and carry him in his arms down to the basement, where he'd make Jake put him back where he'd found him. Then make him throw him in the furnace. Then throw Jake in after him.

"Who went to SU?" Mr. Kleiner said.

Jake's throat was jammed. He shook his head.

"Syracuse!" Mr. Kleiner sneered. "Their basketball team is pitiful this year. Their coach should be working in Kmart. If they'd hire him." Mr. Kleiner laughed. His mouth opened, his forehead wrinkled and cracked like the sidewalk. "You're the newsboy, aren't you? I didn't get my morning paper. And don't tell me you delivered it, because it wasn't there. You got a paper in that bag?"

Jake shook his head again. He knew he was going to be killed.

"Don't expect me to pay for what I don't get," Mr. Kleiner said.

The elevator reached the lobby. The doors opened. Jake waited for Mr. Kleiner to release him from his stare.

"You kids getting off," Mr. Kleiner said, "or do you want to come to the basement with me?"

Connie grabbed Jake by the arm and they darted out through the lobby and into the street. "Close call!" Connie said.

Jake still couldn't talk. They were around the corner when Connie said, "Where's the bag?"

Jake looked down, dumbfounded. He'd left the bag on the elevator. With Mr. Kleiner.

He ran back, with Connie right behind him. The elevator doors were shut, and the indicator pointed to the cellar. They went down the stairs, but when they got to the cellar the elevator had gone up again and they ran back again up to the lobby.

Mr. Kleiner was standing by the doorman's station. The bag was on the desk. Jake tried to fade away. He wanted to sink into the wall.

"You, boy!" Mr. Kleiner pointed a thick, paralyzing finger at him. "You have trouble remembering things, don't you?" He picked up the SU bag and held it like a football. "Here," he said, and sent it spiraling across the lobby.

Jake caught it, wrapped both arms around it, and ran for the door. Five yards. Ten yards. Not exactly a touchdown, but his father would have been proud of him.

SEVENTEEN

Simple Arithmetic

On the street Jake kept looking back, half expecting to see Mr. Kleiner coming after him. They were on a side street, out of sight of their building, a quiet street with not much traffic. Trees grew out of squares of dirt cut in the concrete. Some had tiny fences around them that said KEEP OUT. All he wanted was to dig a little hole and put the dog in and cover it over. But where? There were warning signs everywhere. CURB YOUR DOG...SCHOOL ZONE...NO PARKING...TOW AWAY ZONE...No sign that said BURY YOUR DOG HERE.

There had to be a place to bury a dog. The best thing

would be somewhere close, a place he could pass and know that Big Boy was there.

"How many animals do you think live in the city?" Connie said. They were standing at the corner waiting for the light. "Just start by counting the animals in our building," she said. "Not even the little things people keep in cages like mice, gerbils, and canaries. Just dogs and cats. Give me your best estimate."

"Fifty."

"Not enough. On our floor alone"—she counted off on her fingers—"there's Nelson, and next-door Pal, and Mrs. Bernstein's two miniature bulldogs, and Casey, the Doberman in 5A. There are twelve apartments on each floor, and I bet at least six of them have dogs or cats."

"That's true." But he wasn't really listening. Where to bury the dog? Everywhere he looked, all he saw was concrete and cement.

"Okay?" Connie held him by his shirt. "Let's say ten dogs and cats on every floor. I'm not counting fish, snakes, turtles, and I still get about two hundred animals. Are you with me, Jake? If there are two hundred animals in our building, and the same number approximately in every other building—"

"The point?"

"The point is, there're a lot of animals in the city. Living animals and dead animals. Did you ever think about it?"

She had her face in his. Big glasses and two unblinking,

135

chocolate brown eyes. He got it. She didn't have to give him a lecture. Too many people. Too many animals. Too little space. Overpopulation. Blah, blah, blah. What he wanted wasn't that complicated. He just wanted to put a little dog in a little hole and cover him over.

Give Big Boy his own little place where he could sleep peacefully. Eternal sleep—that's what some people said dying was. But others thought it was just temporary. And who could say who was right? If there really was reincarnation like Lucy said, maybe Big Boy would have a better chance of coming back if he wasn't burned up into nothing in an incinerator.

A corner lot where two streets came together caught Jake's eye. It was just a fenced wedge of dirt. Nobody could ever do anything with it. It was nice loose dirt. It wouldn't be hard to dig a hole. He found a place to squeeze through between a wall and the end of the fence.

Connie worried. "A fence means stay out. It means private property."

"I know what fences mean." Fences were just something in the way to get over, around, or through. He was almost all the way in when he got stuck. Connie tried to pull him back.

"No, push me in," he said.

"What if you get in and you can't get out?"

A woman across the street, behind the window of a little restaurant, banged on the glass, yelling something Jake couldn't hear. She wore a white apron and an orange cap.

"Pull me out," he said.

Connie pulled. She was breathing hard.

Now, there was a man next to the woman. He wore a white apron and an orange cap, too. He came running out, holding a stick. "Private," he yelled. "Private! Private!"

"Pull!" Jake said.

Connie grunted, pulled, and he came free like a cork coming out of a bottle. They both fell down.

The man was still yelling. Jake held up his father's sports bag. "No problem," he yelled back, "no problem. Mistake, mistake. Sorry." He walked away fast.

• EIGHTEEN •

Construction Site

"You guys want a free dog?" Connie said to a couple of boys walking by.

The boys went wide around her with a look that said, *Nobody gives anything away for free in this city.*

"Lost the chance of a lifetime," Connie called after them.

"Cut it out," Jake said.

"What?"

"I don't want you to say anything about the dog."

"Who are you to tell me what to say?"

"The dog's not a joke."

"Who says he is?"

"You do. You're always making jokes."

"Well—that's true, I do joke a lot. I can't help it."

A loaded dump truck shedding dirt and bricks came slowly up the block. "I thought you loved dogs so much," he said. He followed the truck, kept it in sight.

"You know I'm sorry the dog died, Jake, but dogs are dying all the time."

"Don't start that again."

"That's me—I never know when to stop. I know how you feel. I'll cry about Nelson if he ever dies. But it is sort of funny when you think about it. My father says everything's got a funny side."

A yellow crane was stretched out along the sidewalk next to a big construction site. In the pit, diesel shovels were scooping up dirt and bricks and loading waiting trucks. The air was filled with dust and noise. Men in yellow helmets were everywhere. "This is it," he said. "It's perfect."

"Too many yellow helmets," Connie said.

"We can come back when they're gone."

"What if there's a watchman?"

He'd figure out something. He watched a driver climb up on the cab of his truck to direct the shovel operator. They signaled back and forth like a couple of ballplayers. The driver raised both arms, and the shovel operator released a bucket of rubble into the back of the truck. The truck shook. A cloud of dust rose.

The driver jumped down into the cab and drove slowly up the incline. Jake waved as he came by, and the driver waved back. Jake hopped on the running board and hooked his hand through the open window. "Hi."

"How you doing, kid? No rides. Sorry, company rules. How about a doughnut?" There was a box of glazed doughnuts on the seat.

"No thanks," Jake said. He looked at the driver. "I need some advice. I have a dog."

"What kind?"

"Mixed breed, I guess."

"That's the best kind of dog to have. What's his name?"

"Big Boy."

"Oh, a big one."

"No, he was little. He died."

The driver shifted gears. "Well, don't worry about it. Take a doughnut. Go on, take one. You feel bad now, but the good part is, you get another dog, and you're going to like that one just as much." He released his brakes. "Gotta go. I see my boss coming. Hop off, kid. Quick!"

Walking along the street, Jake shared the doughnut with Connie. "That place wouldn't have worked anyway," he said. "Even if I buried him there, they'd just dig him up tomorrow. I'd never know where he was."

• NINETEEN •.

Dead Dog Diddly

Jake was hungry as a bear. It was the pizza smell, and the smell from the bagel shop next to it. Plus the Japanese takeout, and the bakery with trays of giant golden muffins in the window.

"Peach muffins—ummm," Connie hummed.

Pizza or muffins? Which one? He couldn't make up his mind.

"Whichever way I point when I open my eyes," Connie said, "that's what we get." She spun around.

"What's she doing?" a woman carrying two shopping bags asked Jake. Connie fell against the woman. "Watch it, buster," the woman said.

Connie buried her face in Jake's shoulder. "Pizza," she whispered. They went in and ordered. "I'll pay," Jake said when the slices came. Jake, the workingman, had money in his pocket. But as he reached for it, he realized he'd left the bag on the street. "The bag!" He'd done it again. "It's gone."

"Gone," she said. She bit off the drippy end of her pizza. A smile started to form on her face. "That's awful."

He ran out and saw two little kids walking away with the bag. "Hey," he yelled. He caught up to them. "That's my bag."

"We found it," one said.

"Oh, yeah?" Jake gave them a fierce look.

"Yeah," the kid said, but he dropped the bag.

When Jake returned, Connie was holding his pizza for him. "You got it back." There was a joke coming on her face. "Too bad. I was just going to call into the six o'clock news. Headline! 'Kid Dognappers Snatch Dead Dog, Demand Huge Ransom.'" She gave him a sideways glance. "Oops, sorry, Jake. Bad joke."

They passed a man sitting on a stoop. There was an open can in a paper bag on the step beside him. "How you kids doing?" He had a blue bandanna around his neck. "You kids from around here?"

Connie kept going—kids weren't supposed to talk to strangers. But Jake stopped.

"What you got in the bag?" the man said. He had a gray, bristly chin and dark, bulgy eyes.

"Nothing. It's a dog."

The man took a sip from his can. "Your dog. Now that's cool. You got your dog in a zipper bag." He rubbed his golf ball eyes.

Connie sat down a couple of stoops over.

"How come you got your dog in a zipper bag all zipped up?" the man said. "How's he supposed to breathe?"

"He's dead."

"A dead dog. Mmmmm. You got a dead dog in the bag." He looked down the street. "That young lady know you got this dead dog in the bag?"

Connie nodded. She took off her glasses and cleaned them on her shirt.

"Dog dies, that's always sad news. Your dog's number got called. Every dog gets issued a number when it's born. People, too. You never know when your number's going to be called. It could be tomorrow, it could be next week, it could be a hundred years from now. But when your number is called, then you win the giant lotto in the sky. What's your name, boy?"

"Jake."

"Jake, that's great. My name is Bo. Bo," he repeated. He hummed it. "Bo—see what a good sound it makes. Bo... here comes Bo flying low." He swung his arms around like a bird. "Did you see that, boy? That was Big Bo the flying crow. What you going to do with your dead dog, Jake?"

"Bury him."

"Dead dog dies, bury him, that's the way. Don't leave no dog lying in the gutter, looks so ugly it makes you shudder."

The man closed his eyes. They bulged like marbles, under his lids. "Dead dog covered with flies. It's *ugly*. I'm glad you're burying your dog. You are doing good. You're helping the people. People feel bad to see a dead dog. You like to see a dog lively."

"I need a shovel and a place to dig," Jake said. He was hoping the man would help him.

"You have a good spot picked out and everything?"

Jake pointed to a nearby lot, empty except for some abandoned cars and trucks.

"Not there," the man said. "Bad place. See that sign?" He pointed to the side of an old truck with four flat tires. A hand-painted sign said ABSOLUTELY NO TRESPASSING. "You like that word? Tres...passing. French word. Do you know you have French words in English? Spanish words. African words. You don't want to bury your dog here. The landlord is too ugly. I recommend you go to the park, the one by the river. Dogs like it there."

Connie was gesturing to Jake to hurry up.

"You find yourself some bushes," the man said, "keep your head down low, then you dig a hole, and you put your dog in it. Then you say the holy words. Holy, holy, holy. 'Rest in Peace.' Then you cover it over. That's all there is to it." He took a swallow from the can beside him.

The man began to sing. "Dead dog diddly...," he sang. "Ooooohhhhh!"

It was a howl, a dog's howl. It echoed in Jake's head like the chords he sometimes struck on the violin. Harsh, scratchy sounds that made his head hurt.

The man had his head back. "Dead dog day, ooooohh-hhhh. What's the dead dog say? Oooohhhhh! Dead dogs tell no tales. They don't wag no tails. They don't run, they don't play. Don't do nothing but be dead all day. Ooooohhhhhhhh!"

"Well, thanks," Jake said, moving away. Connie was farther down the street. "It's been nice meeting you."

The man slapped his knee. "Jake, you're a triple-play threat. Good-looking boy, a burying party, and super-polite. You get my vote for the all-American, all-star team, for sure."

• TWENTY •

River Park

Jake and Connie walked toward the river with the bag suspended between them on a broomstick they found in the street. The dog had begun to smell. The bag slid one way and then the other. When it got near Connie, she sent it shooting back toward Jake. He didn't think the smell was *that* bad.

"Ooooohhhhh!" The song lingered in his head. He imagined that Big Boy's spirit, the dog spirit, hovered nearby, waiting to see where they were going to put its body.

A group of tourists with cameras and maps crowded them off the sidewalk. The river came into view, bridges and tugboats, everything flat and glittery all the way to the other shore.

"Let's go down to the water," Connie said.

"If you're thinking what I think you're thinking, the answer is no. I'm not going to do it."

"You don't know what I'm thinking. Can you read my mind?"

"I'm not going to throw him in the water, Connie."

"I didn't say 'throw.' You could leave him in the bag. It will be like a boat. We'll put it in the water very gently, Jake, and he'll just sail away."

He imagined the bag riding the long swells out into the current, bobbing in the wake of passing barges. The gulls would find it and tear the bag open with their yellow dagger beaks. "No," he said.

"He'll be in the ocean. You'd like that, wouldn't you, Jake?"

"No."

There were more people in the park than Jake expected: walkers, bikers, kids on skateboards, babies in carriages. Three guys next to the pedestrian bridge drummed on plastic pails. And a girl played a tune on a silver whistle. Gulls squawked overhead. The river made smacking-sucking sounds as it rose and fell among the rocks.

"Do you believe in reincarnation?" he said.

"I do," Connie said. "That's what I mean. Maybe Big Boy will come back as a fish, or a dolphin. Maybe a seagull. Maybe all seagulls were once dogs. Did you ever think of that? Every time you look up and see a seagull, you'll say, 'There's Big Boy.' You could wave to him. And if he saw Mr. Kleiner—"

"—he could drop a present on his head," Jake finished.

That put him in a better mood. He bought a couple of ice creams from a vendor, and they watched a baseball game for a while. The pitcher had good height and a good enough motion: foot up, arm back, and then a long stride forward.

He wondered if his father had found a team yet. What if nobody wanted him? No way. Jake didn't even want to think that. Dave Estabrook was a baseball player. He'd always been a baseball player. Baseball was his whole life. It was something he had to do. It was like an obsession for him. Maybe the same way Jake had to bury a dead dog that wasn't even his. A dog obsession.

"My father is way better than that pitcher," he said to Connie.

"Someday, I hope I get to see him play." She sounded respectful.

"Sure," Jake said, "when the team comes east."

"When's that going to be?"

"I have to check with my father." He said it like it was a sure thing. "When he calls me."

148

They found a place to dig near the fence, where the park edged the road and it wasn't so crowded. The grass was uncut and papers stuck to the fence. Jake put the bag down. He kicked at the grass, then stabbed at the ground with the broomstick. It broke. Connie picked up the broken piece. "Two sticks are better than one," she said.

They worked together. The ground was hard. They chopped at it and scooped the dirt out with their hands. "How deep do we have to go?" Connie licked her lips. Her face was sweaty.

"Two feet," Jake said. He didn't know.

Connie stepped into the hole. "Two feet in the hole. Okay, we're done."

He stepped in next to her. "Four feet."

"You're standing on my feet." She shoved him. He shoved her back. "This is getting weird," she said.

They chopped some more, then Connie went off to find water. Jake worked on. *How am I doing, Big Boy? Do you like this hole I'm digging for you?*

"And what do you think you're doing?"

Jake looked up. The sweat in his eyes blinded him. All he could see was the glitter of a car wheel.

"I'm talking to you." A park cop was sitting in a small one-man vehicle. "What are you digging that hole for?"

Jake wiped his hands on his pants. "I was going to cover it up again."

"You've got that straight, buster. You're going to do it right now. This is a park, junior. You want to dig, go to the sandbox with the little kids."

The cop waited till Jake kicked all the dirt back into the hole. Then he made him stomp it down hard. "Now move." He sat there and watched Jake walk off.

TWENTY-ONE

The Bridge

"What did he say exactly?" Connie asked. They were standing at a water fountain. Jake drank and drank. Then he let the water run all over his face and into his eyes and mouth. "I was watching the whole thing," she said. "Was it scary?"

They walked over to the river. "It was okay. I did what he said, and he let me go." He didn't want to tell her he'd been scared.

"You were so cool," she said. "You were perfect."

"Perfect? He told me to stop digging. I did. He told me to throw the dirt back in the hole. I did. He told me to jump on it and stomp it down. I did. I did what he said. I didn't do anything 'perfect.'"

"That was the genius part," Connie said. "You know how to follow orders."

He leaned on the railing and looked out over the water.

"Don't act so gloomy," Connie said. "We can dig another hole."

He didn't want to dig another hole. He was tired of digging, he was tired of thinking about the dog. Everything seemed hard. His father not playing. His father not coming home. And where was he going to bury Big Boy? Why was he even trying? He was probably crazy or something. He wished he'd never heard of the dog, or Mr. Kleiner, or Howie Silva's newspaper route.

He held the bag over the railing. All he had to do was drop it. *Good-bye, dog.... Go in peace.... Holy, holy, holy. Oooaaahhh! Come on, hand, let go.* But his hand wouldn't do his bidding.

"Jake." Connie pointed to her watch. "I've got to go home, Jake. My mother's going to have a fit. You coming?"

"I can't. I've got this dog."

"Will you be okay?" He followed her over the pedestrian bridge to the other side of the highway. "Where're you going to go now?" she asked. "You sure you're going to be okay?"

"Maybe I'll go to Coney Island."

"Coney Island? You're nuts, Jake."

"My father says there are only three things worth

anything in New York City—Yankee Stadium, Shea Stadium, and Coney Island."

He remembered that it had been a long train ride. He remembered how he used to kneel by the window and look out, and how he knew they were almost to the last stop by the smell of the ocean. There were rides along the boardwalk, and swirly cotton candy, and sandy beaches that stretched for miles.

Connie walked him to the subway. "You know I'd go with you if I could, Jake, but I can't. My mother worries."

"It's okay." He heard the train and ran down the stairs.

• TWENTY-TWO •

The Train

As soon as the train started moving, Jake fell asleep. He dreamed he had Big Boy hidden under his jacket. The dog was poking his head out, and Jake was pushing him back. "Hold it, Big Boy, wait," he said in the dream, "we're almost there."

He woke and found the car full of people. He licked his lips. He'd been sleeping with his mouth open. A mother and her kid pushed in next to him on the seat. The boy sat on his mother's lap and kicked Jake. "Stinky," he said, and held his nose.

Jake moved. He opened the sliding door and crossed to the next car. People moved away from him there, too. He went back and stood between the cars where there was nobody, just the train roaring down dark, windy tunnels. He gripped the guard chains. Lights flew by, the tracks clicked and flashed beneath his feet.

He hummed into the wind, letting his voice rise louder and louder. "Big Boy," he sang, "don't be afraid, I won't let you go."

• TWENTY-THREE •

The Boardwalk

Jake smelled the ocean before the train reached the last stop. He stood by the door the way he had when he was little.

He was the first one out when the doors opened. The elevated platform stood high over the street. He felt like he was up in the sky. He went down a long flight of stairs and out onto the crowded, busy street.

The aroma of sauerkraut and hot dogs mingled with the seaweed reek of the ocean. He saw faces he didn't recognize, boys in identical puffy black and red jackets and hard, grinning faces. His heart was going a little fast. There could be muggers here. They could be anywhere.

When he was in third grade, he'd been mugged by some older kids almost every day for his milk money. He never told his mother. You had to give them something, then they left you alone.

He was hungry. The ocean air always made him hungry. He bought himself a long Coneydog with everything and gobbled it down. He was going to hold on to enough for his train fare home, but then he bought another Coneydog, fries, and a drink, and used up all his money.

He walked toward the ocean, taking the same street his father always had. He burped a lot. He'd eaten too fast.

He remembered how his father would rush to the beach, walking fast and pulling off his shirt. "Breathe, Jake, suck it in. Now, that's air." Then his father would run and Jake would do his best to keep up with him. Once—he must have been really little—he'd lost his father, and when he looked up he was holding another man's hand. The man smiled at him, and a moment later his father showed up.

A Ferris wheel cast a dark shadow overhead. At the end of the block was the beach and the boardwalk that ran alongside it. Sand spilled out into the street. A ramp led up to the boardwalk, but underneath it was all sand. He could bury the dog here. A street sign on the side of a building said SURF AVENUE. It would help him remember the spot.

He went under the boardwalk. Above, people passed, unaware of him. It only took him a moment to scoop a hole out in the sand—it was that easy. The setting sun appeared from under clouds, bars of light fell across the sand. And then the muggers came. He caught a glimpse of cropped heads and puffy jackets. He sprang toward the ramp, but not fast enough. They jostled him and tore the bag from his hand.

By the time he was on his feet, they were fanned out across the boardwalk, running. Without thinking, he ran after them. They jumped a rail and ran across a huge empty parking lot. He saw them stop at the far end of the lot, look back, and then open the bag. They never even looked inside. They just gagged and screamed and threw it away.

TWENTY-FOUR

The Rocks

Jake buried the dog by the ocean at the end of a long rocky jetty. There were several of them, long stony fingers sticking out into the ocean like a hand trying to calm the water.

He found a place to dig above the waterline and buried Big Boy in the SU bag, then covered it with sand and rocks. Squatting there, he listened to the waves hiss toward him across the rocks. The waves came and came, but they never reached him. This was a good place.

Afterward, Jake walked along the water's edge near where he'd buried Big Boy. He was alone. The waves moved restlessly one way and then the other. It had been a long day. All day he'd carried the bag, and now he felt its absence. But he was done.

He remembered the way the muggers had torn the bag from his hand. They thought they had a treasure, but when they opened the bag, all they got was dead dog. He wished he could see it again, see them gag and scream. He hoped they'd thrown up their guts when they ran away and puked all over themselves.

Big Boy would appreciate that. He had liked scaring people. That had been his job when he was alive. Probably he got up every morning and thought about who he was going to scare that day. Just the way Jake got up and thought about the papers he had to deliver, and his father felt his arm and thought about the game he was going to pitch.

A gull landed on the sand nearby, then rose with something in its bill. It was getting dark all along the beach. A girl came toward him, slipping a little in the sand. He thought for a moment it was Connie. Then he thought he heard Big Boy's sharp insistent bark. He slapped his feet down hard on the sand, so Big Boy would hear and remember the sound of his feet.

He watched the waves. They came and came. They never ended. Why couldn't everything be like that? Why couldn't good things go on and on? He followed a wave out, then ran back as the water flooded in over the sand. "Stop!" He turned and ordered the waves to stop, but he had to keep retreating. He couldn't stop the waves. He couldn't stop anything. He wasn't God. He was just a kid.

159

But he still wanted things to be the way he wanted them. He wanted his father to have a great career. He wanted his parents to like each other and live together. He picked up a stick and threw it out over the water. They weren't going to, but he still wanted it.

Water slid and hissed over the sand, and there was a constant soft murmur of wind and water. He drew a long curvy line in the wet sand with the point of a stick. Then he knelt and drew little circles around shells and stones and bits of glass, and bigger circles around his footprints. The biggest circle was the sun, and he made it bristle with rays shooting out of it. Smaller ones were planets, a half circle was the moon, and spirals were the stars. He drew rockets and spaceships, and there was Big Boy in his own spaceship. He drew a long line, ran Big Boy's spaceship out, out, out. "Good-bye." He held his hand up—a farewell, but also a greeting, a salute. "Big Boy, you were a good bad dog."

The ocean heaved up in long smooth hills, rose and rolled toward Jake in glassy silence. He kept his hand up, let the wind play with his fingers. The waves spilled over the rocks and slid into the shore. The ocean came up to where he was standing, wet his sneakers, then raced away.

TWENTY-FIVE

The Police

At the train station, Jake went through his pockets again. He had some change, but not nearly enough. The woman in the change booth was watching him. She had a broad, unfriendly face. He looked for money around the booth. Sometimes people dropped things. Once he'd found twenty dollars in the street.

A man walked by. "Excuse me," Jake said. "Could you lend me a token?" The man went on. Above, on the platform, the trains kept coming and going. He thought of asking the woman in the booth to let him through the gate. He'd pay her back. Instead, when he thought she wasn't looking, he jumped the turnstile.

He ran up the stairs, praying the train was waiting, but the platform was empty. After a while, a policeman came up and took him by the arm and led him downstairs. The woman in the change booth stared at him.

On the street, a policewoman sat behind the wheel of a patrol car. They put him in the backseat. A metal grate separated the front of the car from the back. "You're in trouble now," the policewoman said.

"Can I call my mother?" Jake felt like crying, but he held it back.

"You can't do anything," she said. "What gives you the idea you can jump the fare? That's stealing, just like taking money out of somebody's pocket."

"I have to go home. My mother's going to be worried."

"What's your name?" The policeman was writing everything down.

"Jake Estabrook."

He told them where he lived, and his mother's name and his father's name. He told them his father was a baseball player.

"What team?" the policeman said.

"The Cougars."

"What team is that?"

"It's not from around here," Jake said. "He was with Kansas City one season."

"What are you doing all the way over here, Jake?" the policewoman said.

He hesitated, but then he told her. "I came to bury a dog and I got mugged."

"They took your money?"

"I spent it on Coneydogs."

"Jake," the policewoman said. "It's illegal to bury an animal in the city. You like to break the law, don't you?"

"No."

"What's your phone number?" the policeman asked. He wrote it down, then called into headquarters. "Check this number for me, Jennene, willya? Find out if she's got a kid named Jake and where he is."

They all sat in silence until the radio crackled and Jennene's voice said, "Someone's in the house—not the mother. A friend. The mother's out looking for the kid."

The policewoman said, "Your mother must be gray with a kid like you! You ever do anything for her? You ever think about her?"

She got out of the car and opened his door. "Get out." She clamped a hand on his shoulder and walked him back to the train station. Jake's legs were rubbery. The policewoman nodded to the woman in the booth, then opened the gate and pushed him through. "Get on that train now and go home."

He went slowly up the stairs to the platform. At the top, he looked back. She was still watching him. He waved his hand a little. "Thanks," he said.

TWENTY-SIX

A Happy Dog

Jake stood by the elevator in his building. A woman and a dog came in from outside, and they all got on together. The dog jumped at Jake. She had short brown hair and round eyes, and she was laughing. A happy dog. The woman pulled her down. "Stop, Phoebe. She's a puppy," she said to Jake, "seven months old."

He loved the dog. It made him feel good to see her. Everything made him feel good. He was so happy to be home.

In the apartment, his mother held his face between her warm hands. "You idiot. Are you all right?"

"I was in Coney Island," he said.

"I know. The police called. What were you doing there?"

"It was Mr. Kleiner's dog—" He stopped. He couldn't explain it now. It was too complicated. "Can I have something to eat?"

While he was eating, Connie called. "What happened to the dog? Did you find a place?"

Jake leaned on an elbow. "Yeah, I did." He moved the sandwich around on the plate. "By the ocean," he said, and it seemed so far away.

Later, his mother brought him a glass of chocolate milk in his room. "Your father called. You didn't tell me he's out of baseball."

"He's not," Jake said. "Did he say that?"

"He's off the team. Jake, don't worry. He'll do something."

"There are probably a lot of teams that want him," Jake said.

His mother sat down next to him. "Jake, nothing goes on forever—not baseball, not anything."

"I know that."

"Do you?"

"Yes."

She looked at him a long time. "Your father's thinking about things. He says he wants to talk to you about it."

He lay down on the bed with his clothes on and looked out the window, thinking about the way he'd toted Big Boy around all day. He'd been mugged. The dog had been stolen twice. He'd been arrested. His eyes closed. He heard the machine roar of the city, the whir of fans and motors. The roar, like the wind at the edge of the ocean, never stopped.

Sleep rushed at him. Maybe the day didn't make a whole lot of sense. To somebody else, maybe, it would make no sense at all. But he'd buried Big Boy, and he'd always know where he was. He was glad, though at this moment he wasn't exactly sure why. Tomorrow, he'd figure it out. It was something to talk to his father about when he called.

GILES' SONG

My name is Giles and I'm a dog—
yes sir, I'm a dog—
& I was made to run free.
I made my break on December 25th, 1994.
I saw my chance & I shot through the door
backed by the blond child yelling
GilesGilesGiles in his raspy voice.
I didn't care—by God I'm a dog
& I was made to roam free!

My friend was walking past by chance
and she said, "Hey, Giles!"
I snuffed her hand once
to let her know I was with her.
With GilesGilesGiles
behind me, I ran straight on & she said,
"Make your break, take off, run free!"
So I did. I'm black & my tail
curls over my butt like a question mark
with a white tip. I limp in my front paw
& my breath rasps in my chest now,
but by God I'm a dog—
I was made to run free!
I made my break from that place
where they tie me up night and day—
by God I got away!
She & I walked down the road
& she waited for me when I took a pee
& I waited for her when she sweet-talked
the whiskery horses in the field.

I drank from the duck pond
& didn't chase the ducks.
I snuffed up every loose scent in the grass.
By God, it's good to be alive & free!

She said, "All I need is a four-legged friend
& a house in the woods
& I'm happy. I'm like you,
I need to make my break & run free."
And she said, "Just once before I die,
I want to look a coyote in the eye."

It was getting dark between the trees
& she said, "OK Giles, let's turn around,"
and we saw something on the road
ahead of us, dog-sized, a dark splash,
there and gone. Who knows what it was?
I've smelled all the smells before
& I didn't know: But by God I know I'm a dog
& it's good to be alive!

We walked back past the house
they keep me in, with headlights catching me in the night.
They yelled Giles! & she said, "Go on now!"
but I ignored them all & I ran free.

'Cuz I'm a dog—
yes sir, I'm a dog—
& I need to run free!
I'm a dog—

yes sir good lord I'm a dog—
I'm gonna make my break
one day sweet lord—
I'll be running free!

Gina Mazer
(In memory of Giles, 1982–1996)

I grew up in a family of writers, so it was natural for me to write and for writing to be encouraged. I have been writing poetry since I was a teenager. I met Giles when I lived in a community in Lenox, Massachusetts. He lived about a mile away and often came to visit and take walks with us, until his owners started to keep him tied up. — GM